FROM ASHES

A Heathens Ink Novel

By K.M.Neuhold

CONTENTS

SYNOPSIS

It started with an anonymous post by someone who didn't want to live anymore. I read it over and over again, unable to get it out of my mind. What if my brother Johnny had posted something like this before he'd taken his own life? Would someone have been able to save him?

"When I was so far down I couldn't even see the light, a stranger reached in to save me"~ Nox

I didn't have anything to live for, until a kind stranger pulled me back from the brink. With physical and emotional scars I have nowhere to turn now but to that same stranger who saved my life without realizing it. But as my feelings for Adam grow, will I ever be anything other than a surrogate for the brother he couldn't save? Am I even worthy of his love?

**From Ashes is the third book in the Heathens Ink series, each book in the series CAN be read as a standalone. This is a steamy, emotional M/M romance with guaranteed HEA

CAUTION: this book contains graphic descriptions of domestic violence and drug use that may be disturbing to some readers.

COPYRIGHT

PART I

CHAPTER 1

Adam

January, 2017

**My birthday was yesterday,
I just turned 21.
I don't think I'll live to see 22.
I don't want to.
~Phoenix**

Two minutes ago I flopped down on my couch, after a long day at Heathens Ink, intent on relaxing. I'd pulled up the *Confessions* App on my phone with the intention of finding someone to text dirty, nasty with for a few hours. It's great for some kinky sexting because it's completely anonymous. This leaves people open to some interesting chats. And it lets me feel comfortable enough to explore the long-hidden aspect of my sexuality, namely my attraction to men.

I'm not sure why I clicked on the Most Recent Secrets tab instead of the NSFW tab like I usually do. Fate maybe? Because now I can't stop staring at this post with my heart in my throat.

This post by a user with the name Phoenix

who posted less than five minutes ago about not wanting to live to see his next birthday. In the back of my mind the question worms its way in. Did Johnny tell anyone he planned to take his own life? If he had, could anyone have stopped him? Can I stop this stranger?

Without another thought I click on the whisper chat icon attached to the post.

Inked: Hey
Phoenix: ......

I hold my breath and watch the little dots bounce across the screen, waiting to see if I'll get a response.

Phoenix: hi
Inked: happy birthday
Phoenix: not that happy, but thanks anyway
Inked: I'm sorry. Do you want to talk about that or would you rather talk about something else?
Phoenix: yeah, not about to sob all over you about my shitty life. So if you messaged me to throw me a pity party kindly fuck off.
Inked: I wanted to say happy birthday
Inked: And that things get better
Phoenix: Thanks. That's nice of you. I wish I could believe things could ever get better.
Inked: What about all the people who would

7

miss you if you died?

Phoenix: No one would care. Sorry not to be all emo on you, but it's true. No one will notice if I'm gone

Inked: I'll care

Phoenix: you don't even know me

Inked: so tell me about yourself, then I'll know you

Phoenix:...

I wait, holding my breath as minutes tick by without a response from Phoenix. Is he ignoring me because he doesn't want to get personal? Or, is he too busy to respond?

Phoenix: sorry about that. My boyfriend...

Inked: your boyfriend? I bet he would care if you died

Phoenix: haha, if anything he might be my cause of death

My heart jumps into my throat as I read the words over several times. I don't even know this person, but the urge to climb through the phone and rescue him from an abusive relationship and a life that feels like a prison overwhelms me.

Me: You don't have to stay with someone who hurts you

Phoenix: it's complicated. I'd better go

Me: Wait! I'm worried about you...
Phoenix: don't be

Don't be. Those two words haunt me all night. As if it's that simple. *Don't be.* I don't know why I'm so worried about Phoenix, but fuck I can't stop wondering if he's okay right now.

Maybe in the back of my mind if I can save Phoenix I'll be able to make up for not saving Johnny, for not even knowing he needed saving.

"You're staring at your phone awfully hard. Are you doing that freaky anonymous sexting you love so much?" Gage, my best friend and roommate, asks me with an eyebrow waggle.

"Yeah," I lie.

That's a much easier explanation than telling him I'm obsessing over some random suicidal person who only exchanged a few lines of text with me.

Gage has been my best friend since we were kids. When my brother, Johnny, died he was the only one who understood the pain I felt over it. I can still remember the funeral like it was yesterday. We only stayed as long as necessary at the cemetery before driving to Johnny's favorite overlook with a bottle of Jack and our sorrows to keep us company.

"I feel like it's my fault," Gage admitted between swigs of whiskey. "Johnny and I were... close, I

should've seen the signs. I should've known. I mean, he had his dark moods, but I never thought..."

"It's not your fault. I'm his brother, if anyone should've known it was me."

"We were together," Gage blurted out. "I'm in love with him...I was in love with him," he corrected himself in a choked voice. "With the age difference I was worried you'd be pissed so I was making him wait for us to tell you until he turned eighteen."

"The age difference? You're only four years apart."

"But, he was sixteen, I'm twenty, it seemed fucked up or something."

I took a deep gulp, trying to wrap my head around the new information. It made sense, but it was a bit of a shock to learn that your twenty-year-old friend was secretly dating your sixteen-year-old brother. Any other time I might have been stunned, outraged even, to find out they were hooking up. But I was too numb to feel anything in that moment. None of it mattered anymore.

"I should've known. I should've saved him." He leaned into my shoulder and began to sob against me.

My own pain overtook me and we cried together for all the things that could've been. We mourned all the things Johnny would never be and all the ways our lives would be void without him.

Even eight years later I can't think about Johnny without my throat tightening, my eyes stinging with unshed tears. Gage never got over him either. He became a shell of the person he used to be, going through the motions without living.

I glance over at my best friend on the couch beside me. I would give anything to see him happy again. I wonder if there's anyone in the world who could put a smile back on his face.

My phone pings with an alert as I step into my bedroom after my morning shower. I spring to check it, hoping like hell it's Phoenix. I can't let my mystery friend succumb to the same fate as Johnny, it would be like failing my brother all over again.

> **Phoenix:** Hey, sorry for all the drama and self-pity yesterday. I'm not usually like that, I was just having a day. Anyway, thanks for talking to me and making my birthday suck slightly less.
> **Inked:** It was no hardship, you seem cool. I'd like to talk with you more if it's okay?
> **Phoenix:** Yeah, I'm down for chatting a bit. Tell me something about yourself.
> **Inked:** let's see, basically me in a nutshell: 28, own my own tattoo shop, devastatingly handsome
> **Phoenix:** and humble, lol.

Phoenix: that's cool you own a tattoo shop, I've always wanted a tattoo

Inked: I love it. What do you do?

Phoenix: I do what I have to do to survive

Inked: It doesn't have to be that way. There's more to life than just surviving.

Phoenix: Well, for me surviving is hard enough. If my addiction doesn't kill me, my asshole boyfriend will.

Inked: You can get away from that fucker and you can get clean.

Phoenix: easier said than done

Inked: I didn't say it would be easy but you don't have to die

Inked: what can I do to help? name it

Phoenix: I don't know, just be my friend

Inked: ...ok, but I'm serious when I say that if you need anything I'm here.

Phoenix: why do you care so much?

Inked: I don't want you to die

Phoenix: why?

Inked: because life is worth it

Phoenix: Not mine

Inked: then make it worth living for

Phoenix: I still don't get why you're even talking to me...

Inked: Will it make you feel better if I have a selfish reason?

Phoenix: kind of

Inked: ...My brother killed himself

Phoneix: I'm so sorry :(

Inked: yeah...it was a while ago, but when they say it gets better with time they're lying.

CHAPTER 2

Adam

I drum my fingers to the beat of the music filtering down the hall from Royal's workspace. Royal is one of the five tattoo artists who work for me. They're my best friends, my family.

I lean back in my office chair and rub my eyes. The one thing I could do without when it comes to owning my own business is expense reports.

I glance at my phone beside me on the desk, part of me hoping for a new message from Phoenix. We've been talking regularly over the past week, and it feels like he's starting to relax a little and open up. Any time I try to talk about his boyfriend or drug addiction he shuts down and suddenly has something important he has to do. But, as long as I keep away from those topics he's happy to chat for hours.

It turns out we share a fucked up sense of humor so we've taken to trying to find the best jokes and memes to send to each other. The other day he sent me a meme that said 'Transformation Tuesday' and had a picture of a baby chick and then a chicken nugget. I snort a laugh remembering it.

When my phone buzzes I jump to check who the new message is from.

My face falls when I see the message isn't from Phoenix, it's from Kira. She's been my on and off fuck buddy for the past few years.

Kira: Hey sexy, it's been a while. Free tonight?

I roll my eyes at her message. It's been a while because two months ago she gave me an ultimatum, make things official or no more booty calls. I chose the latter because Kira is as crazy as she is hot. And, as everyone knows, crazy chicks are bomb in bed but you don't want to wife them.

Me: We can hang, but nothing's changed for me so if that's still what you're looking for it's better if we don't complicate things
Kira: That's ok, I just miss you. Lady Persia misses you ;)

I snort and shake my head. Did I mention she's crazy? Proof positive; she named her pussy Lady Persia.

Me: alright, come over around eleven?
Kira: Can't we at least get a drink first?

I sigh and pinch the bridge of my nose. I have

no doubt she's going to have a few drinks, start rubbing up against me, and then tell me I have to be her boyfriend to hit that. Fuck that, it's *so* not worth it.

If I'm being honest I'm over everything to do with Kira. She's a hard ten and the word 'no' isn't anywhere in her vocabulary. On occasion I've tried to come up with crazy shit to suggest to her in bed just to see where her limit is, and she never flinches. I've fucked her in ways that most people have never dreamed of. Better yet, she never batted an eye when I've asked for things I probably wouldn't have had the guts to ask someone who was more inhibited. But, we've had our fun and I think it's time to move on. I at least owe it to her to tell her to her face that I'm over it.

Me: K. O'Malley's at eleven?
Kira: Can't wait

A knock at my office door makes me jump.

"Come on in," I call out, setting my phone back down on my desk.

Gage peeks his head in. His dyed green hair is sticking up in all directions.

"Hey, wanted to see if you wanted to grab some lunch?"

"Yeah, totally. Can you give me five minutes to finish this damn spreadsheet?"

"Sure," he nods and disappears again.

My stomach twists as I stare at the space where my best friend just disappeared from. Is it even fair to call him my best friend when I've been keeping a huge secret from him for over a decade?

The familiar panic rises in my chest as my train of thought continues down that path. I never meant to hide such a major part of myself from Gage, and the rest of the world, for so long but things got out of hand.

When I first realized I was bisexual I didn't know how to feel about it and I wasn't ready to tell anyone because, frankly, it was confusing. It could be argued that when Johnny came out to me when I was seventeen, that would've been a good time to come out to him as well. But I didn't. And a short time later when Gage came out, I still wasn't ready. I knew I was being a coward, but I didn't want to be forced to come out before I felt like the time was right. Then Johnny died.

Johnny was always emotionally fragile. He was four years younger than me and undeniably the baby of the family. It drove me fucking insane when we were kids and my mom babied the shit out of him. As he grew into his teen years he was a loner, one of those kids who spent all his time listening to depressing music and lamenting how pointless everything was. I think we all figured it was normal teenage angst. None of us knew he was being bullied at school. None of us knew he was self-medicating with any pills he could get his hands on. None of us knew he planned to take his own life.

I rub my chest against the tightness that always seems to manifest when I think about Johnny. If I'd told him I was bisexual would he have been more open with me about what a hard time he was having? Could it have saved his life to know he wasn't alone?

And that's the crux of why, eight years later, I still haven't told Gage I'm bi. He loved Johnny. I didn't know it until after Johnny was gone, but Gage was absolutely crazy in love with him. There's no way Gage wouldn't blame me, at least partially, for Johnny's death if he knew I was bi and never told him or Johnny when it mattered the most.

Pushing away my dark thoughts I turn back to my dreaded spreadsheet and enter the last few figures I need and then total it before saving.

I stand up from my desk and stretch my arms over my head, letting out a groan as my muscles tug and my bones crackle into place. Closing in on thirty and I already feel like an old man.

I check my phone one more time for any messages from Phoenix, and when I don't see one I pocket it and head up front to go out with Gage.

"So, what's it going to take for me to see the ink you're hiding under that tight shirt?"

I scowl when I hear the rude come-on from the front of the shop.

"A better pick-up line, some manners, and some shampoo. Better luck next time," Dani, our main piercer and token bad-ass woman of the shop, easily rebuffs the douchebag.

I can't blame the guy for trying. Dani is stunningly beautiful and fierce as hell. If I didn't see her as a sister I'd be begging her to give me a chance. And I know for a fact that if most of the other guys who work at Heathens were straight they'd be fighting over our girl.

It didn't occur to me before now, but out of six people working at Heathens- including myself- only one person is totally straight. Nash, Royal's best friend and roommate is the one straight guy, and I'm not even convinced that he isn't at least flexible or curious because I'm fairly sure there's some underlying sexual tension between him and Royal. And Dani mostly dates guys, but she's made a point of telling us that she doesn't like labels and she doesn't care about gender. So, maybe no straight people are working at Heathens.

"Ready to go?" I ask Gage, peaking my head into his work space.

He sets down his sketchbook and stands up.

"Want to grab burritos from that food truck up the street?"

"Fuck yeah," I agree, mouth-watering at the thought.

"You're buying," Gage tells me with a wink.

I give him the finger and laugh good naturedly. I don't know what I'd do without Gage. He's a brother to me. I just hope that one day when I work up the balls to tell him I've been lying to him for fifteen years, he can find it in his heart to forgive me.

After a long ass day at Heathens all I really want to do is go home and crash out in front of the T.V. Maybe watch some *Tattoo Nightmares* and see if I can get Phoenix on messenger. Instead I'm shoving through the Friday night crowd at O'Malley's trying to spot Kira.

I startle when a pair of slender arms wrap around my waist but when I look down and notice the fingernails are painted with an elaborate design and a little heart tattoo on the left wrist- done by yours truly- I know it's Kira.

I turn my head and force a smile.

"I'll grab our drinks if you can find somewhere to sit?"

"On it," she agrees, giving my ass cheek a pinch before sauntering off with a swing of her hips.

A few minutes later I'm sliding into a booth and passing Kira a peach sangria.

"Thanks, love," she purrs, putting her hand on my knee and scooting close.

I decided the best course of action would be to wait until Kira has a few drinks in her, and then I'll tell her things are over between us, put her in an Uber, and pray she lets it go without having a major meltdown. That's the thing about

Kira, she's a spoiled brat. The crazy really comes out when she doesn't get her way. One time I tried to end things with her and she faked a pregnancy. I found out the whole thing was a scam to get me back when I overheard her friends laughing about it. And now I'm wondering how I let her lead me around by my dick this long to begin with.

"How've you been?" Kira asks, brushing her long, dark hair over her shoulder and leaning toward me so I get a good view of her ample cleavage.

That trick has always worked in the past to send my mind instantly to the gutter, remembering nights when I've lubed up and fucked her tits until I came all over her neck. My dick can't seem to muster it's normal enthusiasm for her, though. Which is further proof it's time to end things for good.

"Not bad." I bring my beer to my lips and glance around at the packed bar.

"I heard Madden was at that nightclub with the shooting, is he okay?"

I narrow my eyes at her. On the surface it seems like she's genuinely concerned about the wellbeing of my friend who was shot, but that's so not Kira. She's the most self-centered person I've ever met, there's no way she gives a shit how Madden's doing.

"He's recovering," I answer as succinctly as possible.

"He should sell his story, I bet he could

make millions."

Annnnd there it is.

"I'll mention that to him," I mutter.

She launches into telling me all about her friends who I couldn't possibly care less about, and my eyes return to roaming just for something to do.

My gaze falls on a man by the bar and my interest instantly piques. He's built like the fucking hulk with muscles so massive I'm positive he could crush me in his fist. And that is hotter than fuck. My heart pounds as my eyes continue to drink in his broad shoulders, my mind conjuring images of the way his muscles would tense and flex under my hands as he fucks me. When I finally make it to his face I'm not disappointed. His strong, square jaw sets off his pouty lips and deep-set eyes.

I wonder what Phoenix looks like. Is he a big dude like The Hulk over there by the bar? Or is he small and slender? Perhaps somewhere in between? What's he like in real life? Sure, online he's wickedly funny and heartbreakingly sad, but in person does that translate? What does his voice sound like? What color are his eyes?

These thoughts chase themselves around in my mind until my hand is twitching toward my phone.

"Are you even listening to me?" Kira demands in a sharp voice.

"Uh, yeah," I lie.

"I'm going to cut right to the chase, Adam," Kira says, reaching for my hand and looking me in the eye. *Here we fucking go.* "I miss you and I think we're good together. I feel like you should reconsider giving us a chance."

"Kira, I'm sorry but I've told you more than once I'm not looking for something serious."

Her eyes narrow and her lips purse as she prepares herself for full tantrum mode. After a second her face morphs into a sweet smile.

"I understand. Can I have one last kiss, for old time sake?"

I roll my eyes but relent. What could one kiss hurt?

I lean in, pressing my lips to hers. She tastes like a mixture of peach sangria and watermelon lipgloss. I relent as she flicks her tongue along the seam of my lips, letting her in for our tongues to mate.

"What the fuck is this?" An angry masculine voice demands to know.

I pull back and wipe the back of my hand across my lips to remove the remnants of lipgloss.

"Can I help you?" I ask coolly.

"Yeah, you can get your fucking hands off my woman."

I quirk an eyebrow at Kira who seems pleased as punch over the development.

"I warned you, Nick, if you didn't get your act together I was going to find someone else."

"Fucking hell, I get it now. This was about

making your boyfriend jealous?" The boyfriend is cracking his knuckles and looking at me menacingly. "Well, this was fun but it seems like you two have some shit to talk about, if you'll excuse me. Oh, and Kira, do me a favor and lose my number."

I stand and try to inch past Nick. But he's apparently determined to start a fight because he steps directly in my path and glowers down at me.

"Dude, I don't give a shit about your girl, you're welcome to her. Now will you please get the fuck out of my way so I can leave?"

I hold my hands up and ease around him without a backward glance.

It only takes ten minutes to get home and as I'm sticking my key in the lock my phone buzzes in my pocket.

I pull it out and smile when I see the icon for a *Confessions* message.

Phoenix: Hey
Inked: Hey
Phoenix: how's your night going?
Inked: pretty crazy actually
Phoenix: ooooo, do tell
Inked: I met up with this girl who's been an on and off fuck buddy so I could break things off with her
Phoenix: Oh? Why'd you want to end things?
Inked: for starters she's fucking crazy
Phoenix: I doubt she suddenly became crazy.

so what's the real reason you decided to end it now if you've been on and off before?

Inked: ...I've never told anyone this

Phoenix: you don't have to tell me anything you don't want to

Inked: I'm bisexual. Obviously this isn't anything new, but lately the itch to try it on with a guy has been getting stronger. Tonight, the thought of fucking her did nothing for me. But I got hard checking out a guy standing by the bar. Sorry if that's an overshare.

Phoenix: Not an overshare. I'm flattered you chose me to be the first person you've told.

Inked: I wish I could tell everyone, but I'll probably lose my best friend when I finally do

Phoenix: if he's really your best friend he'll stand by you

Inked: I hope so

Inked: Can I ask you something?

Phoenix: sure

Inked: Can I see a pic of you?

Phoenix: ...

Phoenix: sorry, no

Inked: :(

Phoenix: I don't look good. Drugs will do a number on your good looks man, believe me when I tell you that

Inked: :(I'll send you a pic of me if you'd like?

Phoenix: if you want to

I hold my phone up and snap a quick selfie to

send to Phoenix.

Phoenix: damn, you're ridiculously hot
Inked: thanks *blushes*
Phoenix: shit, I've gotta go my bf just got home
Inked: ok...take care of yourself

The feeling of a tight fist around my gut is becoming a familiar one when I get done chatting with Phoenix. I'm constantly worrying any time could be the last, eventually the messages just won't come again.

CHAPTER 3

Adam

"You're looking awfully chipper," Royal, one of my tattoo artists, accuses.

"I'm always chipper," I respond with a cheeky grin.

"Right, of course you are." He snorts a laugh and I give him the finger. "Oh, I get it, you were all up in Kira's nasty snatch last night, weren't you?"

I cringe at his crude language. Royal's not exactly the think before you speak type so I've gotten used to his particular way with words.

"First of all, there's nothing wrong with Kira's *snatch*, as you so eloquently put it. And no, we didn't hook up last night. I told her I'm over it."

Royal rolls his eyes.

"I've heard that one before. Well, whatever's got you in such a good mood, I hope it lasts."

"Thanks man, me too."

"Ready to go home?" Nash, another of my artists and Royal's best friend and roommate, asks Royal as he emerges from the back.

"Yeah, I just want to veg out and watch some movies or something."

"Cool. Order a pizza?" Nash throws an arm

over Royal's shoulder and I don't miss the look of longing that passes over Royal's face.

Royal's been in love with Nash forever. The problem is that Nash is straight, or at least straight-ish. Who knows, maybe they'll find their way at some point. I'm rooting for them.

Nox

"Thanks, you were good," the guy says dismissively as he stands from my bed and pulls his jeans back into place. I don't even know his name.

He reaches into his pocket and pulls out a small wad of bills.

"Over there is fine," I nod toward my dresser.

He sets the cash on top of the dresser, pulls his shirt on, and leaves without a backward glance.

My skin crawls with a familiar feeling, the throbbing emptiness in my chest only serving to double my need for relief, for escape.

I roll over and grab my jeans off the floor. I reach my hand into the front pocket and come back with a small handful of assorted pills. Without concern for what they are I toss the whole lot into my mouth and swallow them dry.

The pills and dope used to stamp down the suffocating loneliness. The desperation to feel something, anything used to be tempered by the drugs.

My phone buzzes from somewhere on the floor.

Inked: Hey Phoenix
Phoenix: Why hello there, Inked. How's it going?

The empty ache in my chest eases a fraction at the emotional contact with someone I've come to consider a friend, even if we've never met or even spoken. It doesn't hurt that he's gorgeous. He's exactly the kind of man I picture when I close my eyes and let myself imagine a life where I'm happy.

Inked: Nothing exciting today. So bored at work I'm looking up anti-jokes and giggling to myself
Phoenix: wtf is an anti-joke? Lol
Inked: What did the farmer say when he lost his tractor?
Phoenix: what?
Inked: Hey, where's my tractor
Phoenix: *snort laugh*, seriously, what the actual fuck?
Inked: hell if I know, it's funny though
Inked: Can I ask you something?
Phoenix: Of course
Inked: What's your screen name mean?
Phoneix: My mom used to always say 'from ashes we rise', made me think of the mythical Phoenix. Just popped into my head when I was

making my profile on this app.

Inked: That's kind of a nice saying. Was there something specific she meant by it?

Phoenix: Who knows, she was high as a fucking kite 24 hours a day lol

Inked: That must've been hard as a kid.

Phoenix: yeah well, life sucks and then you die. No big deal, I survived.

Inked: I wish I could do more for you. I wish you'd seriously consider coming out to Seattle and letting me help you. I'll wire you the money for the plane ticket.

Phoenix: I told you last time we talked, I'm not taking your charity

There's an odd, warm tingle along my skin at the very idea that someone like this sexy, successful man with his shit together gives a fuck about someone like me. Is it possible for me to take a chance at a new life?

The hole I've found myself in feels too deep to climb out of, but here's this perfect stranger reaching in and trying to pull me out. But can he bear my weight or will I pull him into the hole beside me?

The walls of my shitty apartment feel like they're closing in on me. The drugs aren't enough to numb the pain anymore. The thought of living this way for one more day is agony. The only thing that has kept me from taking a straight razor and dragging it across my wrists is Inked.

I don't understand why but he gives a shit about whether I live or die. At least he seems to. For some inexplicable reason I don't want to let him down. I want to find a way to crawl out of this pit of despair rather than succumb to it. But fuck if that doesn't sound like the most insurmountable task. I'm the spider in the sink, scrambling for a foothold, but inevitably being pulled down the drain.

Phoenix: Have you ever woken up in the morning and just wished you didn't have to anymore?

Inked: Please talk to me. What's wrong?

Phoenix: Everything is wrong. I feel like I can't fucking breathe. I can't take it anymore.

Inked: I want to help you. Please tell me how I can help you?

Phoenix: I'm not sure there is any help for me

Inked: I don't mean to sound like a broken record but I'll buy you a plane ticket. Come out to Seattle, I'll help you get clean, I'll do anything to make sure you're ok. It's not charity I swear.

Phoenix: I'll think about it

Inked: Please let me help you

Phoenix: You've helped me in more ways than you know. I think I need to figure out a way to help myself now.

Adam

I stand outside a well-kept two-story house just outside of the city, waiting for someone to answer the door.

It only takes a few seconds for the door to swing open. A large man with a friendly smile greets me.

"Adam, good to see you again," he says, holding his hand out to shake.

"Ditto, man." I step inside and look around. It looks as nice inside as it did from the outside which eases some of the anxiety I've been having lately over Madden staying here.

A little over a week ago my employee, friend, and roommate Madden was shot during a hate incident at a gay club downtown. He met Thane, the owner of the house I'm currently standing in, that same night.

I met Madden a few years ago when he was a homeless junkie who stumbled into Heathens looking to sell some sketches. No doubt he planned to use the money for dope. I looked at the skinny, twitchy kid in need of a hand up in the world, and I saw Johnny.

I offered Madden an apprenticeship on the spot with the catch being he was never to touch drugs again. To my surprise, he accepted. He's been a good friend and a good employee ever since.

After the shooting his leg wasn't in any

shape for our fifth-floor walk-up, so Thane offered for him to stay at his place where there was a spare bedroom on the first floor. This is the longest Madden has been out of my sight in years. Maybe I'm a little over protective of him, but he always seemed fragile to me. Or maybe I'm projecting Johnny onto him again.

"Hey dude," I greet Madden as I walk into the living room and find Madden on the couch.

I slide down onto the couch cushion beside Madden and he winces. I immediately feel awful. I can't imagine the amount of pain he must still be in.

"Let me get you some Tylenol," Thane rushes to offer when he notices the pain in Madden's expression.

"Yeah, thanks," Madden grits out.

His face turns in my direction and I can't stop myself from quickly assessing him, looking for any signs that he might be taking the Oxy he was prescribed at the hospital.

"Don't worry, it's plain Tylenol, no codeine," Madden assures me.

"Are you doing okay with...everything?" I ask. I can't imagine how difficult it must be trying to heal but not being able to take your pain meds.

"Yeah, haven't touched the shit the hospital sent me home with."

"What about everything else?"

Thane returns with a glass of water and two extra strength Tylenol. I watch as Madden gives Thane an adoring smile. A niggle of jealousy worms its way into my chest. Not over Madden, he's like a brother to me. But the thought of having someone to care for you, and to care for in return...it sounds *nice*.

"I'm alright. I'm healing little by little, Thane's taking good care of me."

"Good. When does your physical therapy start?"

"Tomorrow, then I should have a timeline for getting back to work."

"Don't worry about that. Your job is there waiting for you, no matter how long it takes. Focus on getting better."

"Thanks, man."

My phone pings with a message and I quickly whip it out, hoping it'll be from Phoenix.

Phoenix: Why don't kleptomaniacs like puns?
Inked: why?
Phoenix: because they always take things literally
Inked: lol! Ok that one was actually really funny
Phoenix: *takes a bow*

"Kira?" Madden asks with a hint of disapproval in his tone.

I know none of them ever got why I fucked around with Kira. I can't explain it myself, other than to say she was hot and the sex was good.

"Uh, no," I shove my phone back in my pocket, still thinking of Phoenix.

We settle back and fall into a comfortable silence as a new episode of *Tattoo Nightmares* comes on.

Nox

Inked: Have you ever felt so lonely it's like a physical pain?

Phoenix: every day

Phoenix: Having a bad day?

Inked: I wouldn't go that far. Just thinking lately about how nice it would be to have someone

Phoenix: ok, describe for me your perfect life partner

Inked: get's my sense of humor, doesn't mind spending a friday night watching terrible movies together, adventurous in bed...basically I want a best friend who I can fuck. Lol.

Phoenix: guy or girl?

Inked: doesn't matter. What about you?

Phoenix: I just want a man to love me

Inked: He's out there. You just need to fight to find him. Don't give up yet.

Phoenix: You're making me want to fight, for the first time in my life.

Inked: Come to Seattle

Phoenix: Maybe

CHAPTER 4

Nox

The sharp bite of the needle as it pierces my skin is a rush in and of itself. My body buzzes in anticipation of the endorphins I'm about to receive. I draw back, heart hammering as a flash of blood appears in the syringe. Then I push the plunger all the way down, my head lolling back as euphoria hits me with the force of a thousand orgasms.

I live for this moment. The one shining second when my brain floods with feel good chemicals. Everything else in my life fades away, if only briefly.

I lay back on my threadbare mattress and let the sensation of floating carry me away. Peaceful waves of ecstasy wash me to a different world. One where I've never used my body to pay for an addiction. A world where I've never had to live in a car and beg for food. A world where I'm some*one* rather than some*thing*. It's funny how drugs can give you such crazy ideas.

"Why isn't there ever any goddamn food in

this house?" Harrison gripes, opening then shutting each cabinet forcefully, as though punishing them for being empty. He goes to the refrigerator next and does the same thing.

The reason for the lack of food is inside the baggies on our coffee table. By coffee table I mean milk crate in the middle of our living room.

"You got any money?" He demands, eyeing me with speculation. I force myself not to cringe under his gaze. There was a time I thought Harrison was handsome. When we first met I was convinced he could be my ticket to a better life.

I remember it like it was yesterday. I was sixteen and living on the streets. My mother had died six months prior and I'd been doing everything I could to simply survive.

I folded my arms over my torso to block some of the frigid November air. A silver BMW slowed to a stop and my heart leapt with hope. If he's driving a BMW there was a good chance I'd be able to afford something to eat after giving him what he wanted. That wasn't always a given.

The passenger window rolled down and I did my best to look enticing as I sauntered up to the window.

"Hey handsome, is there something I can help you with tonight?"

That was my first glimpse at Harrison's dark eyes and firm jaw. His wolfish expression should have frightened me, but instead it sent a thrill of excitement through me.

"I think I could find a use for a man like your-self."

Man was a stretch, even I knew at sixteen I was barely more than a child, while he appeared to be more than twice my age.

I opened the car door and slid into the heated leather seat. My ass warmed instantly.

"Heated seats? How fancy."

"How much for the rest of the night?"

"Two hundred."

He reached into his pocket and flung a stack of bills into my lap. I counted it with shaky hands, having to go back and re-count twice before I was able to believe what I held in my fist. Three thousand dollars.

"You're mine until morning. You're going to enjoy yourself." It wasn't a promise, it was a demand. I refused to think about what he might expect for so much money. "I had a bad day at work and I want to get fucked up first so we're going to a party."

After that night Harrison became a regular. I didn't see him every week, and sometimes he'd go months at a time without showing up. But he always came back. He told me I was his favorite toy.

A year ago, after a long stretch of not seeing him, Harrison showed up seeming to have something different in mind. Instead of picking me up for a night of sex and drugs, he suddenly wanted to wine and dine me, buy me lavish gifts, and treat me like I mattered. It worked in his favor that I was at the lowest point I'd ever been in my life, contemplating suicide daily.

A few weeks before Harrison showed back up in my life, my best friend Amanda Viecelli was murdered.

I met Amanda when we were both fourteen working the same corner to pay for food or, more often, drugs. She understood what it was like to have been dealt a shitty hand at life and have to do anything necessary to survive. When my mom overdosed and I was all alone Amanda took me in, showed me the safest places to bunk down for the night and which soup kitchens had the best food. She was like the sister I never had.

I knew something was up when I didn't see her around her usual spots as often. Then, the rumors started that she'd been spotted with a rich new boyfriend and didn't have to sell her ass for dope anymore. I'll admit, I was more than a little jealous.

Less than a month later I heard that they'd found her body floating in the Chicago River. Rumors ran rampant all over the street from strangulation to accidental overdose to decapitation. The last one made no sense to me, because how would anyone have known it was her if she didn't have her head? People don't always use common sense when they're making shit up. However it happened, my best friend was dead. And as soon as the police found out she was a working girl they didn't put so much effort into finding out who killed her.

So, when Harrison showed up and swept me off my feet I was in desperate need of comfort and willing to do anything for him.

It wasn't long before he was paying me enough that I didn't need to work the corner to support my habit. I even lived nicely for the first time in my life. I started spinning a fairy tale in my mind with Harrison the Edward Lewis to my Vivian Ward- if Julia Roberts had been played by a man, obviously. I missed all the signs of Harrison falling into the same drug laced trap I'd been in since the age of twelve. At the end of six months we were living in my apartment together, selling our furniture for drug money.

I went back to selling my dignity for dope.

My phone pings with an app alert.

"That's why we don't have food, because you spent the money on a phone to call your fuck buddies," Harrison sneers.

"At least my asshole is a source of income," I mutter under my breath.

I don't see Harrison's fist coming until it's too late to duck.

"Worthless fucking whore," he spits as I pick myself up off the floor, right eye already starting to swell. "I'm going out." He stuffs the baggie of dope in his pocket and storms out the front door. *Fuck, there goes my fix.*

I don't dare open my mouth. If he goes out I might have peace for the night. Slinking onto the couch I check my phone. My heart flutters when I see it's the nice guy I talked to the other night on the *Confessions* app.

> **Inked**: hey, how's your week going?
> **Phoenix:** fucking peachy :/ you?
> **Inked**: meh, can't complain. Been thinking about you.
> **Phoenix:** lol, what were you thinking about me?
> **Inked**: That I told you about me, but you didn't tell me anything about yourself
> **Phoenix:** I draw
> **Inked**: sweet! Can I see?

Warmth spreads through me. No one has ever asked to see my art. I get to my feet and take my phone with me to my bedroom closet. I sift past the pile of clean clothes, behind a few boxes full of random junk we picked up to sell, and grab my sketchbook. I snap a picture of a cherry blossom tree I drew last week. Then I take a picture of my 'Real Life in Chicago' series, a drawing of a cold homeless man. I attach both pictures in a message and hit send. As soon as it's done my stomach roils. I've never shared my art before and I don't know why I did now.

When my phone pings with his next message I'm almost too afraid to look. I'm sure he thinks my art is shit. How could he not?

Inked: Holy fuck, those are amazing. I'm speechless right now.

Phoenix: thank you *blushing*

Inked: Just putting it out there that if someone showed up at my shop with these sketches looking for a job, I'd hire them as an apprentice in a hot second.

Phoenix: *rolls eyes* Not if they were a junkie

Inked: wouldn't be the first time. If you ever change your mind it's Heathens Ink in Seattle, WA

I allow myself to dream for a second about a life where I create permanent art instead of...whatever this is.

Adam

"Hurry up, man," Gage calls through my door.

"I'm coming," I grumble as I tug on a pair of jeans.

I've been dreading this all week. And dreading it makes me feel guilty. It's not that I don't want to remember Johnny on his birthday. And it's not that I wouldn't do anything to help Gage cope. The problem and the thing I dread is my parents.

I step out of my room and find Gage leaning against the wall opposite my bedroom door, waiting for me.

Gage is holding a bouquet of wildflowers exactly like he had every March 28th for the past eight years.

"Ready to go?"

"Yeah, let's get this over with," I agree.

Gage frowns.

"You could show a little more respect for his memory."

"Jesus, I think I show proper deference for my dead brother. Excuse the fuck out of me for hating these awkward goddamn dinners with my alcoholic mother and emotionally absent father. Fuck," I snap and then feel immediately shameful for it. "I'm sorry, I know this sucks for you too. I didn't mean to take it out on you."

"It's okay, I get it."

We ride in silence to my parents place and when we get there Gage goes around the back, to the gazebo in the backyard, while I head to the front door. I don't know what the significance of the gazebo was to Gage and Johnny, I've never asked. But every year he goes back there and leaves the flowers before joining us inside.

The front door swings open before I reach it and my mother stands there looking pale and thin.

"You're late," she accuses, a slight slur in her words.

"Sorry, mom. We hit traffic."

"Some way to honor your dead brother."

I clench my jaw. I want to yell at her that

I honor Johnny every damn day. I commemorate him by helping others avoid the path he traveled down.

"Sorry, mom."

She nods, seemingly appeased, and then steps aside to let me in.

I step into the living room where my dad is watching a basketball game and notice the shrine they've built to Johnny has expanded. Every time I visit there seems to be a new picture or item displayed.

"Hi, dad."

He grunts but doesn't bother to look in my direction. My heart aches for the father I lost the day Johnny died. For the mother I lost too for that matter. In one fell swoop I lost my entire family and my best friend. Could Johnny have had any idea how far his choice would reverberate in our lives? Did he even once think of what it would do to us?

My phone vibrates in my pocket and I pull it out, my heart leaping when I see it's a message from Phoenix.

Phoenix: Hey, whatcha up to?
Inked: Visiting my parents...it would've been Johnny's 24 b-day today :(
Phoenix: I'm so sorry.
Inked: thanks. The worst part is how my parents are now. We used to be close. They were so great when we were growing up. Now

They're like empty shells. Gage is too. And then I wonder if there's something wrong with me that I managed to keep living when Johnny died and they couldn't. And sometimes I hate him for what he did to us. I feel bad, I shouldn't hate him.

Phoenix: I think he would understand your anger. And I don't think there's anything wrong with you. You're all doing your best to deal with it. Everyone handles these things differently.

Inked: Thank you. It feels good just to have someone to blurt that stuff out to. I can't tell anyone else I feel that way sometimes. No one else would understand.

Phoenix: I bet they'd understand more than you realize. But I'm glad to be here for you to word vomit on too.

Inked: Lol. Gross. I better go before my mother decides texting is a blight on Johnny's memory. Talk to you later.

CHAPTER 5

April 2017

Inked: What's white and can't climb trees?
Phoenix: ?
Inked: a refrigerator
Phoenix: *groan* truly a terrible joke
Inked: What do you call a deer with no eyes?
Phoenix: no eye-deer lol
Inked: no, it's still just a deer, the absence of eyes doesn't change the animal
Phoenix: there should be a law against these crimes against comedy

Phoenix: I would kill for a chocolate chip cookie right now
Inked: Get some
Phoenix: ugh, can't. No money. The bf takes my money for dope, and then complains there's no food in the house.
Inked: I hate hearing how he treats you. You're so fun and amazing. You're one of my favorite

people in the whole world. I want you to be happy and safe. I want to know you're cared for

Phoenix: Stop, you're going to make me cry. This is my life, Inked.

Inked: It doesn't have to be. Tell me something you dream of. If you could have anything in the world?

Phoenix: A mountain of chocolate chip cookies lol

Inked: smartass

May 2017

Inked: I just saw the hottest guy at the grocery store. We reached for the same brand of garbage bags at the same time. It was a serious love connection

Phoenix: lol, you're a dork.

Phoenix: So, what did he look like? I'm dying to know what type of guy you go for

Inked: why? Hoping you're my type? ;) lol

Phoenix: obviously. Now tell me!

Inked: alright, I guess I like guys who are a little on the small side, kind of lean muscle. I kind of go for the innocent, cute looking kind of guys. But, at the same time I want someone with substance. Someone who's lived and struggled and come out the other side strong and full of wisdom.

Phoenix: wow. I was expecting like "tattooed

beefcake"

Inked: nah, then it'd be like I'm dating myself ;) lol. Not that I wouldn't want a guy with ink.

Inked: So...what's the verdict, are you my type? Lol

Phoenix: that's for me to know and you to find out

Inked: find out??? Does that mean you're coming?!

Phoenix:...sorry....I was just being flippant. I still don't know, Inked. I'm not sure yet. I told you there's a lot of things to think about

Inked: what's there to think about? Leave your shithead boyfriend and come let me take care of you. I'll buy you a bus ticket, I'll pay for your rehab. I don't understand what's to think about.

Phoenix: Everything! You don't fucking get it. I have to go. Ttyl

Inked: Wait!

Inked: Phoenix, I'm sorry. Please

Phoenix: It's fine, but I do have to go. Later sweetie XX

Phoenix: Hey

Inked: Holy shit, you worried the hell out of me! Where have you been?!

Phoenix: BF got mad and smashed my phone.

Had to squirrel away money for a new one
Inked: I thought…
Inked: I was so worried.
Phoenix: I'm sorry. I didn't mean to worry you sweetie. I promise I'm fine. Well, as fine as I ever am.
Phoenix: I missed you. Tell me a stupid joke
Inked: What's worse than finding a worm in your apple?
Phoenix: what?
Inked: The Holocaust
Phoenix: oh my god that joke is awful, and possibly offensive lol
Inked: lol, how is it offensive? The Holocaust is *way* worse than a worm in an apple
Phoenix: fair enough. Tell me about your place. I want to pretend I'm there with you.
Inked: you don't have to pretend. You could be here.
Phoenix: please, sweetie, just describe it to me

June 2017
Nox

Looking around at our living room filled with strangers in varying states of fucked up, Inked's words ricochet around my brain, reminding me that maybe my life doesn't have to always be this way. In fact, I've made up my mind. I'm getting out. I'm done sucking dick for heroin. I'm done shooting poison into my veins to make life bearable. *I'm done.* Which is why I've already been scoping out rehab facilities. I have a bus ticket tucked away in my underwear drawer for tomorrow afternoon. This is my last hurrah.

With well-practiced motions I wrap my cellphone charger around my bicep to act as a tourniquet. The bite of the needle as it pierces my skin is it's own heady rush. I know what comes next. Just this one last time and then never again. I pull back on the plunger of the syringe and watch it fill with blood, before injecting the poison straight into my veins. *Instant bliss.*

The noise of everyone in the room around me blurs as everything fades into a pleasant haze and euphoria washes over my body.

"What the fuck is this Nox?"

I blink slowly at the words directed at me, trying to decipher their meaning, or even who spoke them.

"Goddamit, you worthless, junkie, whore."

Suddenly I'm being dragged off the couch by my hair and all of the commotion in the room stills as everyone stops to see what's about to happen. Not that any of them would care to stop him from hurting me. These people are here to get high, not worry about domestic violence.

"You think you can fucking leave me you stupid piece of shit?"

My bus ticket flutters down to the floor beside me and the fog clears from my brain a little as I realize what's happening. I always knew that he would let me leave him over my dead body, quite literally. I lay flat on my stomach with Harrison looming over me, panting with rage.

I was so fucking close to getting out. But I guess I always knew it wasn't meant to be. I was born the bastard child of a useless, junkie whore. And now *I'm* going to die a useless, junkie whore. It's kind of poetic when you think about it.

The click of a lighter meets my ears and my drug addled brain tries to put the pieces together. Before I can manage, I realize that I'm way too hot and something smells like burning meat. An unholy scream pierces my eardrums before the world goes black around me.

Adam

I check my phone for the thousandth time today, still no messages from Phoenix. I last heard from him two days ago..

I've sent him three messages and all have gone unread.

"You're awfully fidgety tonight, are you okay?" Gage asks.

"I'm fine," I lie, checking my phone again.

My mind won't stop feeding me scenarios. Phoenix dead with a needle in his arm. Phoenix beaten to a bloody pulp by his boyfriend. Phoenix sitting in a jail cell. Phoenix giving up all hope and letting himself fall into the abyss.

Inked: You're really worrying me man. Please

let me know if you're okay. If you're in trouble come to Seattle. I'll help you. I'll send you money for a plane ticket. I care about you. I need you to be okay. Fight for yourself. Fight for hope. Please, please don't give up.

PART II

CHAPTER 6

Nox

August 2018

I'm trembling from head to toe as I stand on the sidewalk across the street from the small tattoo parlor. *Heathens Ink.*

What am I doing here? This is such a huge mistake. *Did I really think coming here to beg Adam for an apprenticeship was a good idea?* My stomach dances with nerves as I try to swallow down the fear.

You have to at least try. I chant in my mind, clutching my sketchbook close to my chest. What's the worst that can happen? *He could tell me no.* I don't have anything now, so I won't be any worse off than I am right this second. *But, you'll have been rejected by* him. The small voice in the back of my mind taunts.

I take another deep breath and pull my shoulders back, forcing myself to appear confident. *Fake it 'til you make it, and all that shit.*

I speed walk across the street and push through the door before I can take another second to talk myself out of it. The tinkling sound of the bell over the door makes my mouth go dry. *What the fuck am I doing here?*

I'm about to turn around and walk right back out when the man behind the counter looks up from the computer, his gaze coming to rest directly on me. I feel the heat creep into my cheeks, but I ignore it and push my shoulders back again. I walk straight to the counter, and as soon as I'm standing directly in front of him... my mind goes blank.

It's *him*. My stomach flutters and my heart pounds out an erratic rhythm in my chest. The trembling worsens to the point that I'm sure he can tell.

I take a second to catalogue his features. His chestnut hair is long and messy, like he simply rolled out of bed and came to work. He has a silver barbell through his left eyebrow, as well as small gauges in each ear. His emerald eyes penetrate me as he takes me in as well.

Crap, I've been standing here staring at him for god knows how long. I clear my throat and force words past my lips.

"Are you the owner?" Of course it is. I'd know him anywhere. I downloaded that picture he sent and looked at it every time I thought about relapsing. He was my strength. He was my reason to do better, be better, hope for more.

He nods and his lips quirk up in a friendly, yet professional, smile.

"Yeah, Adam," he says offering his hand.

"Are you here for some ink?"

I give a small shake of my head and slide my portfolio onto the desk.

"I'm here for a job."

He eyes me curiously for several seconds before reaching for my portfolio and pulling it toward himself.

"I've never tattooed before, but I think my artwork speaks for itself," I offer with feigned confidence.

He flips my portfolio open and I hold my breath as he begins to peruse it. I've never let anyone see my art before, except for my counselor in rehab...and the one time I sent Adam a picture of two of my drawings. It's a bit like standing naked in front of him, to have him viewing my art. No, this is more nerve wracking than standing naked. Hell, I sold my ass for a while to pay for my addiction, I feel more vulnerable in this moment than I ever did then.

"These are good," He says, continuing to flip. My heart flutters with nervous hope as he pauses on the colorful phoenix drawing. "These are really damn good."

He closes the book and looks up at me speculatively. I clench my fists to hide the shaking in my hands and I hold my breath, awaiting his judgement. Then, his gaze lands on my arms and I can only imagine what he must be thinking as he takes in my old track marks and the careful, even scarring of cuts that were clearly intentional, and then the rough, raised skin where my flesh was nearly melted away.

"I'm clean," I blurt in a hurry.

I know most people don't want to take a chance on a former junkie, but I need this so fucking badly. Adam nods slowly and meets my eyes. When he does his lips part in surprise and his brows furrow.

He blinks and shakes his head slightly, like he's trying to clear his thoughts.

"Alright, here's the deal. I'll give you an apprenticeship. You'll also run the front desk and do some cleaning around the shop several hours a week that I'll pay you for. If I have any reason whatsoever to believe you're using, you're out. Got it?"

I nod enthusiastically and smile.

"Yes, absolutely."

"Okay, I'll see you back here tomorrow at nine in the morning and we'll get your employment paperwork taken care of."

"I can't thank you enough, you have no idea what this means to me."

"Wait," He calls out. "I didn't catch your name."

"Lennox, you can call me Nox."

"Nox" He repeats. My name on his lips sends a small shiver down my spine.

"Good night, Adam."

"Night, Nox."

Adam

I can't tear my eyes away from Nox until he disappears out of sight, leaving my brain spinning like tires trying to gain traction on an icy road.

A recovering junkie with a beautiful phoenix drawing in his portfolio. It can't be *him*, but still it feels like fate.

The second I laid eyes on him it had felt like an electric volt going through my body. He's the most beautifully broken man I've ever seen in my life.

"You know, you don't *have* to adopt every gay drug addict who walks in off the street and gives you puppy dog eyes," Gage says, startling me out of my musings.

"Oh, please, Dad! I promise to feed him and walk him. I'll clean up after him when he makes messes," I mock plead.

"You joke, but you know that's exactly what's going to end up happening."

I frown, annoyed at Gages condemnation.

"At the end of the day it doesn't matter if you approve or not. It's my shop, my decision."

"That's right, it's your world and we're all just living in it." Gage storms toward his work station and I follow him.

"You know that's not what I meant. I lost my fucking brother and if helping strangers is how I need to deal with that then back the fuck off and let me deal with it." I snap, hands shaking with pent up rage.

"That's the problem, you act like you're the only one who lost Johnny. When he died he took my goddamn heart with him. And you parading guys through here to replace him doesn't help," Gage shouts before whirling around knocking his sketchbook to the floor to relieve tension.

"I'm sorry," my voice softens. "I'm not trying to hurt you, I'm just doing my best to cope."

"I know, I'm sorry, too." Gage's shoulders sag, his eyes meeting mine with hesitation.

"Come here, asshole." I pull him into a hug and clap him on his back. "Let's close up and go home."

Gage nods in agreement and we set about our closing routine.

I don't know if I would've been able to build Heathens Ink to where it is today if it hadn't been for Gage. Only a year after Johnny's death Gage was hardly functional, but when I told him there was an opportunity to buy this building for way under market value and open the tattoo shop I'd always dreamed of, he was all in.

He threw himself into helping me with everything that went into renovating and getting Heathens off the ground. He was there with me building up our client base from the ground up. He was there for me when I was sure this whole stupid dream couldn't have been a bigger mistake. He's as much a brother to me as Johnny was.

As I head out the front door for the night

there's a strange fluttering in the pit of my stomach that I can only place as excited nerves. It can't possibly have anything to do with looking forward to seeing more of my new apprentice. Absolutely not.

Nox

I stand in front of the mirror in my motel room and take in my outfit one last time. I hardly slept last night, too excited about starting my first respectable job today. The idea of being around Adam all day didn't help either. I know I shouldn't want him. And, I'm sure he has a beautiful, perfect girlfriend, or boyfriend, who's never had a heroin addiction or had sex for money. But, that doesn't stop me from hoping, just a little, that maybe one day...

I hardly recognize myself anymore, in a good way.

After the ... *incident*, I woke up in the hospital after a two week long medically induced coma. I had second and third degree burns on my forearms, stomach and chest. Apparently I'd had the wherewithal to roll over and smother the flames and someone had the conscience to call an ambulance. No one had the balls to name Harrison, though. The story told by everyone questioned was that I was so high I accidentally lit myself on fire. With only my own drug clouded version of events Harrison walked free.

The one good thing that came out of it was

during my medically induced coma, during which time they began to treat my burns, I was also fortunate enough to bypass the worst of detoxing.

When I walked out of the hospital a few months later, after several skin grafts, I walked right into a rehab center to make sure I wouldn't slip back into my old ways.

Now here I am: out of rehab and clean for the first time since I was fourteen. I have a job and the possibility of a future in front of me. And I owe it to Adam, but he doesn't even know it. There's no doubt in my mind I would've taken my own life, or let Harrison do it for me, if Adam hadn't befriended me and pulled me out of the darkness.

My skin has a healthy glow I've never seen before, my hair is no longer dull and limp. And, there's life in my eyes I hardly recognize. This is my new beginning.

"You can do this. Compared to everything else you've gone through this is fucking cake," I tell my reflection sternly before heading out to face my first day.

Adam

I drum my fingers against the desk in my office trying to place the root of the restless energy coursing through me. Maybe it's because I haven't gotten laid in ages. In fact, the last person I fucked around with was Kira and that was...holy god, that was a goddamn year ago.

My mind wanders to Phoenix. I never heard

from him again and I can only imagine what that must mean. My stomach twists at the thought of it. Yet another person I failed to save. It's like letting Johnny down all over again.

A light knock on my door pulls me out of my thoughts.

The door creaks open and the lust that courses through me, seeing Nox for a second time, is like a punch in the gut.

A shy smile plays at the corners of his lips and has me instantly hard as granite.

I gesture for him to come in, clearing my throat and shifting in my seat.

"Is this a bad time?" he asks, glancing between me and the door. I take a deep breath and try to relax the tension coursing through my body.

"No, this is fine."

I slide the employment paperwork toward him and he sets to work filling it out. My eyes roam over his long fingers as he writes and then along the marred skin of his forearms. What happened to him? The insane urge to pull him into my arms and soothe any pain of his past, rushes over me.

Jesus, get a grip man. He's an employee, I can't come on to him or I'll have a sexual harassment lawsuit on my hands. Besides, he clearly has baggage being a recovering addict and all. The last fucking thing I need is another damaged man to obsess over.

My door creaks open again and Madden peeks his head in.

"Madden, what's up?"

If anyone had a more difficult year than I did last year it was Madden. But he finally recovered from the shooting both physically and mentally, and found a deep, amazing love with Thane. I couldn't be happier for him.

In fact, love seems to be going around the shop because, as I suspected, Nash and Royal finally got their shit together and stopped dancing around each other. The surprising part was that they came together with another man between them...or however they've worked out the dynamics of their poly relationship, I haven't asked for any specific details.

Now I just need to get Gage, Owen, and Dani paired off and I'll be all set. Then I'll be the only lonely bastard here.

"I was going to run across the street for some coffee, do you want anything?" Madden asks, pulling me from my thoughts.

"Yeah, that'd be great. Do you want anything, Nox?"

He looks up from the paperwork and then glances over his shoulder at Madden.

"I'd love a small, black coffee, if you don't mind."

"No problem," Madden says with a friendly smile.

Once the paperwork is done I show Nox

around the shop and introduce him to everyone. He seems nervous at first but starts to relax as the morning wears on.

When lunchtime rolls around he pulls out a sandwich and his sketchbook and makes himself comfortable in our makeshift breakroom. I sit across from him arguing with myself about whether he wants me to shut the hell up while he sketches or if he'd be open to conversation.

I get lost in watching him as his features relax once he's absorbed in his art. Nox sweeps his hair off his forehead absentmindedly. When I look down at what he's drawing I notice he's working on the phoenix he showed me as part of his portfolio. It's stunning, so vibrant and somehow gives the feeling of a true rebirth. And, of course, reminds me of my lost friend.

Royal walks up behind Nox and pauses as he gazes down at the sketch and then at Nox's hands.

"Feel free to tell me to fuck off, but what happened to your arms?"

Nox tenses visibly and stops drawing. My breath catches as I watch the pained expression flit over his face before being replaced by an emotionless mask.

"A fire," he answers quietly.

"Damn," Royal mutters.

Nox shifts uncomfortably in his chair.

"Sorry," Royal mumbles, finally aware of his faux pas.

"No, it's okay," Nox assures him with a fake

smile.

"What was it like?" Royal blurts. Seriously, I'm two seconds from knocking him out.

Nox lets out a humorless laugh.

"Well, if you have to go through it I'd recommend being high off your ass on Heroin. It really takes the edge off."

Royal opens and closes his mouth several times and I stifle a laugh. What he went through was clearly not funny, but the fact that he can joke about it is impressive as hell.

And, suddenly the phoenix makes more sense.

"You want that inked on you?" I ask, gesturing to his drawing.

"Absolutely, once I can afford it."

My heart sinks a little. Of course he's struggling financially. He's a recovering addict, for all I know this is his first real job. I shy away from the thought of what he might have done to support his habit.

"If you're going to work at a tattoo shop you need ink. We can consider it like a uniform allowance," I offer with a smirk.

Nox tenses again and eyes me suspiciously.

"You don't want *anything* in return for it?"

My stomach lurches. Fuck, the assumptions I was trying to avoid must have some weight to them.

"No, man. In fact, this is mostly selfish on my part. That's an incredible sketch and I want to make sure it's done justice."

He glances down and looks at the sketch for several seconds before nodding cautiously.

"That sounds awesome, thank you."

"Don't mention it."

CHAPTER 7

Nox

By the end of my first day I'm exhausted. But, it's the good kind of exhausted. It's the kind of tired you feel when you've put in an honest day's work. I've never felt that before.

"Hey Nox, you want to come grab a drink with us at O'Malley's?" Royal offers as we're all cleaning up and closing up the shop.

I duck my head in an attempt to hide my blush, but I'm sure he can see it anyway.

"I...don't drink," I offer the bare bones excuse that I'm hoping will suffice. I did joke to him earlier about heroin, but I doubt he thought I was serious about my problem with addiction. Or maybe he did, who knows.

"That's okay, you can still come hang out. It'll give us a chance to get to know you," Royal insists. "Plus, there's a really hot bartender who swings both ways." He waggles his eyebrows and smirks.

"Hey, if anyone is hooking up with Beau it's going to be me," Dani argues.

Dani seems to be the only woman working at Heathens, but can undoubtedly handle herself among all the rowdy men who call the shop home.

I glance around at everyone looking over at me hopefully. They really do seem like a great group. There are six people working here aside from Adam. Gage seems to be the most standoffish of the group, and Adam's best friend. Gage is tall, well over six feet, with blue dyed hair and sad eyes. He gives off the distinct impression of a piece of glass that's full of cracks, bound to shatter at the slightest touch.

Then there's Nash and Royal, from what I can tell they're a couple but it seems to be fairly new, and they've mentioned a third man several times which frankly is pretty hot, and hopefully when I get to know them better I can weasel some salacious details out of them.

Owen was the newest employee before I showed up. He had only been at Heathen's for six months and seems pretty reserved compared to most everyone else. I get the feeling he's got some demons of his own.

Finally, there's Madden. Madden has the air of someone who's been to hell and back and lived to tell the tale.

It's cool as hell that pretty much everyone at the shop is queer. Although, I'm not supposed to know that Adam is bi and I'm certainly not going to let that slip to his friends.

"Alright, why not," I reluctantly agree.

Dani loops an arm through mine and begins steering me toward the door.

"Yo, boss man, get your ass out here it's closing time," she shouts as she flips the sign on the door to 'closed'.

The sound of Adam's office door opening makes my stomach flutter. I need to get a grip on this stupid crush. Just because he was nice to me over the internet when he thought I was suicidal doesn't mean he could ever be interested in a guy like me.

Throughout the day numerous gorgeous women came into the shop to see Adam. And, it was obvious by their blatant flirting they were looking for more than a tattoo.

"You do realize that you're not supposed to talk to your boss like that, right?" He teases as he makes his way out of the shop, turning off lights as he goes.

"I didn't think you'd want to miss drinks at O'Malley's."

Adam glances at me briefly and I let a sliver of hope into my heart that maybe he's hoping I'm coming out with them tonight. Then again, he knows about my addiction problem, maybe he was glancing at me because he's worried about me going to the bar.

He nods briefly before following us out of the shop.

O'Malley's is only about a block away from Heathens so we decide to walk over. Dani loops her arm through mine once again and keeps up a constant stream of chatter the entire walk. Once we arrive at the bar Dani drags me toward the bar top and our group claims the whole row of stools.

"Beau, get us a round of lemon drops please," Dani calls out before turning to face me. "Oh my god, I just noticed your eyes. They're so gorgeous."

"Uh...are you hitting on me? Because I don't swing that way."

Dani laughs.

"Kinda figured."

"Are you saying I *look* gay? That is offensive, darling," I joke.

After about an hour at the bar, the shot placed in front of me when we arrived is taunting me. The longer I stare at it the more tempting it looks. I never had a problem with alcohol. Would it really be the end of the world if I have one drink?

"You alright?" Adam's warm breath on my neck makes me shiver and suddenly the alcohol isn't so tempting anymore.

"Yeah," I nod and push the drink away. "I'm pretty tired though, I think I might call it a night."

"I didn't notice your car parked at the shop."

"No, I don't have a car at the moment," *or ever,* "I'm staying within walking distance."

Adam's brow furrows. He reaches into his wallet and pulls out several bills, placing them on the bar before standing up.

"I'll drive you."

"You don't have to, really it's not far," I argue. I don't particularly want him to see the hourly rate motel I'm staying at.

After the *incident* a local domestic violence group collected money to help me get on my feet. The last thing I want to do is run through it and have to go back to my old ways of getting by.

"It's not a problem. Gage, you staying out for a while or riding with me?"

"I'm fine for now," Gage answers.

Without another word Adam places a gentle hand on the small of my back and steers me toward the exit. A thrill dances in every nerve ending at the brief, yet protective contact. No one has ever cared about my well-being before. Myself included.

Once outside we walk the short distance back to the shop without exchanging any words. When he leads me to a shiny, red mustang my eyes nearly pop out of my head.

"This is a gorgeous car."

Adam smiles proudly, opening the passenger door for me. My heart skips a beat at the gesture. I thought that was something guys only did in the movies.

"She's my baby," he remarks, as he lovingly strokes the door while I climb in.

"Do the two of you need a few minutes alone?" I tease.

Adam gives me a sardonic smile before making his way around to the driver side of the car.

Adam

When Nox said he was staying somewhere within walking distance I was immediately suspicious. The only place I could think of close by the shop is an hourly rate motel known for prostitution and drug activity.

"It's right up there," he announces, pointing at the exact motel I was afraid it would be.

Instead of pulling in I shake my head and continue to press my foot down on the gas pedal.

"Adam, what are you doing?"

"You're not staying there," I say through clenched teeth. There's no way in hell I'm dropping him off at that place. Might as well toss him to the lions.

"It's all I can afford. Don't worry I'm not doing drugs or anything," he argues.

"I've got an extra room, you can come stay with me. Gage lives with me, and Madden used to also, but he lives with his boyfriend now. It doesn't make sense for you to throw money away staying at a dump like that when I've got a perfectly good, empty room."

"Adam, that would be weird. We don't even know each other. And I don't want to be your charity case."

His words hit me in the chest, reminding me of Phoenix and how I let him down. I should've pushed harder. I should've offered to go there and get him instead of just inviting him to come to me. I should've done so much differently.

I sigh and glance over at him.

"It's not charity. Like I said, Gage lives with me and Madden used to, also. Even Dani stayed there for a short time when she started at Heathens. I've got space and I like to keep a close-knit group at the shop. When one of my employees need help I'm there. Always."

Nox huffs and crosses his arms defiantly. I almost want to laugh at him for acting like a petulant child, but I doubt that would convince him to come stay with me.

"Fine, but you need to go back so I can get my stuff."

I nod and find a place to make a U-turn, doing a mental fist pump that I won.

Nox

It didn't take me long to gather the few things I had from the motel. Now I'm standing in Adam's extra bedroom, my new bedroom, trying to decide what to do with myself. I can't believe I'm here in Adam's house. Thoughts of simply meeting Adam are what kept me going through most of rehab, now I'm his roommate. How's that for surreal?

A light knock on my door makes me realize I'm still just standing in my bedroom in the clothes I wore to work and the bar. I feel kind of grimy with stale cigarette smoke that lingered in the air from decades of patrons smoking at O'Malley's.

"Yes?"

"I was wondering if you want to watch a movie or anything?"

A smile creeps over my lips as I break out in a little happy dance. He wants to *hang out* with me.

"Nox?"

I stop dancing and put a hand over my mouth to muffle the giggle that escapes me. Giggling, seriously?

"Yeah, just give me a few minutes to get changed," I call out.

"Okay."

I open my tattered suitcase, another donation from the domestic violence charity, and sift through my clothes. I pull out a pair of loose sweatpants and a t-shirt.

When I step out into the living room, Adam's eyes flick over me like a caress. His gaze lingers for several seconds on how low the sweatpants ride on my narrow hips. I blush and tug at my shirt when I realize the raised scars of my stomach are showing. The motion seems to break Adam's trance. He clears his throat and tears his attention away from me.

"What's your favorite movie?" He asks, logging into his Amazon account.

"*American Beauty.*"

"No way," he argues with a shake of his head and a chuckle.

"What, my favorite movie isn't good

enough for you?" I challenge with a mock glare, giving him a playful shoulder shove for good measure as well. I'm a little rusty with my flirting, so sue me.

"No, it's a good movie. But a *favorite* movie is one you could watch every day. *American Beauty* is too dark, if you watch that movie too much you'd kill yourself."

Or maybe my life is so dark that movie doesn't seem so bad. I bite my tongue to keep from saying these words. Adam doesn't need me dumping my shit on him.

"Fine, what's your favorite movie then?"

"Anchorman," he answers with a shrug. I roll my eyes and he laughs. "Alright, if you like the dark stuff I've got one for you."

He pulls up a movie called *Donnie Darko* and quirks an eyebrow at me. I wave my hand at him to go ahead and put it on and we both settle in to watch.

Adam

I glance over at Nox out of the corner of my eye and clench my jaw against the urge to strip those low-slung pants off and run my tongue all over his cock. My attention wanders upward and latches onto the scarred skin peeking out where his shirt rides up. I'm dying to know more about what happened, but it's probably better if I don't launch into an inquisition on night one.

Without conscious thought, I reach out and

run a gentle finger against the raised skin on his exposed shoulder. Nox shivers and glances over at me.

"I'm sorry," I say, clearing my throat and pulling my hand back.

"No, it's okay. It felt… nice," he licks his lips and I have to bite back a groan. Probably best if I don't touch him again.

"If, uh…if I have scars on my back too, will the skin be too damaged for my tattoo?"

I sit forward to get a better look.

"May I?" I ask, ghosting my fingers along the exposed skin. Nox nods breathlessly and I pull the back of his shirt up to see the extent of the damage. "Is it your whole back?"

"Not my whole back. And, it's not as bad as on my stomach and my arms."

The unexpected urge to trail my lips over his vandalized skin punches me in the gut.

"It's possible but the texture could pose a major problem and if there was nerve damage the tattooing process will be extremely painful. Not to mention, with scarring this severe there's a high chance that the ink will bleed. There are only a few rough spots so I think we can work with it, but I want you to know what you're getting into. "

"I'm not worried about pain and if the ink bleeds then it bleeds."

"Okay," I agree.

"When?"

"It'll take a few sessions to finish, but we can

start tomorrow after we close up shop if you like."

He nods eagerly before settling back on the couch to turn back to the movie. My hopes of paying any attention are completely blown by the raging hard-on I'm sporting knowing that I'm going to get his shirt off tomorrow and have my hands all over him. *I'm so going to hell.*

The front door opens and I jump back from Nox like I've been caught with my hand in the cookie jar.

"Uh...hey," Gage greets, looking between Nox and myself with confusion.

"Hey, Nox is taking Madden's old room."

Gage tenses momentarily but doesn't say anything. He gives Nox a friendly head nod before heading for his room without a word.

I know it's directly my fault, but the fissure that's developed between Gage and myself over the past year is like an open wound, painful and impossible to ignore.

CHAPTER 8

Adam

When we get into Heathens the next morning I ask Dani to show Nox all of the computer stuff while I set up my station for my first appointment. Less than three minutes later Royal is standing in my station with that shit eating grin on his face again.

"I noticed you and Nox drove in together this morning."

I grunt in acknowledgment and continue mixing colors. Seeing that I'm not giving him what he's looking for he decides to change tactics.

"He's hot."

I open my mouth to respond when it occurs to me that this is a trap. Last year I slipped up and sort of implied to Nash that I have some interest in men. Whether Nash would've shared that with Royal, or if Royal picked up on something on his own, I'm not sure. But the way he's looking at me right now, studying my reaction, I'm sure he's suspicious.

I settle for a shrug.

"He needed somewhere to stay, Madden's old room was sitting empty."

"Are you sure that's all it is?" Royal asks, his tone gentler this time.

"He's my employee, and he's clearly got a lot on his own plate right now as it is," I reason, not bothering to pretend that his gender is one of the problems.

"It would be okay to let yourself be happy, you know."

He doesn't stick around to wait for me to argue or bluster.

The day flies by in a blur as I try to focus on my work instead of the fact that when the shop closes tonight I'm going to get my hands on Nox's bare skin. I'm going to put my mark on him.

Once everyone else is gone and the shop is closed Nox and I head back into my studio.

"I haven't set up yet because I wanted to show you the process," I explain as we step into my spotless work area. He nods and sidles close to me so I can show him how to set up.

Once I'm set up he strips his shirt over his head and drapes it over the spare chair. My eyes roam over the expanse of skin before me. The scars are even more substantial than I would have guessed, but it doesn't detract from his beauty. He's real and raw, his body is *lived in*.

My throat tightens and my heart pounds with sheer awe, imagining the things Nox must've been through in his life, and how strong he must be to have emerged on the other side.

He twitches under my gaze and runs a hand along the marred skin of his lower abdomen.

"Sorry," I apologize, clearing my throat and forcing my attention away.

"I know, it's kind of gross to look at," Nox's voice is small.

"No," I say with vehemence. "You're beautiful."

The words are out before I can filter myself. Nox's eyes go wide and a faint pink creeps into his cheeks.

"Thank you," he says in a near whisper.

I shift in my seat to adjust my erection. *Christ, I need to get a grip.*

"How do you want me?" Nox's tempting words have my mind diving straight back into the gutter. I clear my throat and pull on my latex gloves before motioning him forward to place the tracing on his skin.

"I figure we can get the outline done tonight and then start working on the color in about two weeks."

Nox nods eagerly, craning his neck to see the sketch now imprinted on his skin from the base of his spine to his shoulder blades.

He was right, the scars on his back are few and not as bad as the ones on this arms and stomach. I wonder for the hundredth time in two days what happened to him.

Once he's settled in the chair I notice a slight trembling in his hands.

"Are you nervous?"

He let's out a humorless laugh.

"Are you asking if I'm afraid of pain?"

"Just because you've experienced a tremendous amount of pain doesn't mean you're eager for more," I argue.

Nox shrugs.

"I'm not nervous."

"Then why are you trembling?"

His eyes meet mine and there's a fire in them that no doubt matches my own. I wrench my gaze away and clear my throat once again, repeating the words over and over in my head; *He's an employee, you promised not to take advantage of him, he's not for you.*

Nox

The low buzz of the tattoo needle sends a shiver up my spine, and thankfully pulls my thoughts out of the gutter, where they've resided all day at the thought of Adam's hands on me.

"When did you know you wanted to be a tattoo artist?" I ask as the first bite of the needle hits my skin.

I wasn't being facetious before about not being afraid of pain. I've learned in my life that pain is all about mind over matter. There's no physical pain that can rival the mental anguish I've lived with, because physical pain is always short lived. The needle inking my skin is nothing.

"I've always been an artist, but I knew I wanted to do tattoo's after I got my first tat," he pauses and swallows like he's trying to decide if he should say more or leave it at that. "It's, uh, in honor of my brother after he...died."

"I'm so sorry for your loss," I say, swallowing the bitter taste of the lie of omission. I should tell him who I am. I know I need to tell him. But how do you even bring that up? How do I tell him that I know his secrets and he knows mine?

He shrugs off my sympathy.

"I suppose I liked the idea of being able to create lasting memories for people, something they could carry with them forever. I love helping people tell their story in ink."

"That's what I've always thought, too. I feel like our scars are like a roadmap of our lives, and a tattoo is a beautiful scar."

Adam nods, his brow furrowed as he concentrates on his practiced strokes with the needle.

"Want to tell me more about your scars?"

"I'd rather not, at least not right now," I answer, swallowing past the lump in my throat.

"Okay. What's your favorite food?"

"Everything," I answer with a laugh.

When you've gone without food for days on end, just knowing you can go home to a stocked fridge at night is a dream come true. Adam must be able to read the pain in my voice because he stops inking and looks up at me with sympathy in his eyes.

"Please don't pity me," I whisper.

Adam nods and returns to the task at hand.

For the next hour and a half Adam meticulously inks the outline of the phoenix on my skin and we stick strictly to light topics of conversation. When he's done he wipes the stray ink and blood from my skin and then directs me to the strategically placed mirrors so I can see my own back.

"Wow, it's going to be so beautiful."

"Yeah it is. This might just be my best work yet." He grins proudly before he starts to clean up his supplies.

"Since you won't let me pay you for the tat, will you at least let me buy you dinner?" I offer as I pull my shirt over my head.

"I never turn down a meal."

I follow Adam into a hole-in-the-wall restaurant. The booths are more tape than plastic at this point, and the walls are slightly yellowed from years of patrons smoking. But, I'll admit it smells like heaven, if heaven smells like onion rings.

"I know it doesn't look like much, but the burgers here are unbelievable."

"I'm not picky," I assure him. "It smells amazing."

After a waitress comes and takes our order a strained silence falls between us. The little voice in the back of my head roars to life, pointing out that Adam deserves to know who I am. He's doing so much for me, I can't lie to him.

"So...uh...there's something I need to tell you," I say before I can chicken out.

"What's that?"

"Well...um...the thing is....what I'm trying to say...."

"Spit it out," Adam prompts with a reassuring smile.

"I'm Phoenix."

Adam looks like he's been slapped. He stares at me open mouthed for at least ten heartbeats. And then, without warning, he gets up and comes around to my side of the booth. He grabs my arm and drags me out of my seat. I cringe, bracing myself to be hit. Instead, his arms wrap around me, pulling me against his chest. His whole body is shaking as he stands there holding me without words.

My own body begins to tremble as well and my eyes burn with emotion. Never in my life has someone touched me tenderly. It feels incredible. Adam's arms holding firm are better than any drug I've ever taken.

"I thought you were dead," he says, his voice strained. "I thought I failed you, just like I failed Johnny."

"I almost was," I admit.

Adam releases me and I bite back a whimper and resist chasing his gentle touch.

"What happened?"

I gesture for him to sit down and take a deep breath.

"I was coming here. I had a bus ticket and a plan to sneak off when I knew my boyfriend would be out of the apartment. I was literally one day from freedom." Adam looks stricken as he reaches across the table and takes my hand. "Harrison found the ticket." I shrug like it was no big deal. Like it wasn't the most afraid I've ever been. Like I didn't barely escape with my life.

"What did he do?" Adam whispers.

"You can't guess?" I hold up my arms as a hint.

"How did you survive?"

"Someone called 9-1-1, I'm not sure who. No one would testify against Harrison. They all said I set *myself* on fire because I was so high."

"Wait, he's not in prison?" Adam gasps in horror.

"Nope."

"Holy fuck. Does he know where you are now?"

"Not that I know of. I haven't seen him since that night. After I got out of the hospital I went to rehab, and then I came here."

Adam's fingers squeeze mine, his gaze intense and worried.

"I'm glad you came here. I'll help you in any

way you need."

"Thank you," I force the words past the lump in my throat. "I don't understand why you took the chance on me, but I can never thank you enough."

"Isn't the first time." Adam shrugs. "Madden was tweaked out of his mind when he walked into Heathens. And, don't tell any of the guys this if it ever comes up, but Owen walked right into Heathens fresh out of prison. We all have our demons. Doesn't mean we don't deserve a second chance."

"You're a really good person."

Adam waves off my words.

"Anyone would do what I do."

"No, they wouldn't," I argue.

"It's not enough to make up for Johnny. It'll never be enough."

A twinge of sadness hits me. Of course this is all about his brother. I'm nothing more than a chance for him to quiet his demons.

He gets a sad, faraway look in his eyes and I know I shouldn't argue. Nothing I can say will absolve him of the guilt he carries.

CHAPTER 9

Adam

Nox is Phoenix. *Nox* is Phoenix. Nox is *Phoenix*. I can't stop looking at him across the table as he devours his cheeseburger like it's his last meal. I guess I'm not *that* surprised Nox is Phoenix. I'm more surprised that Phoenix is alive and sitting before me. I've spent all year believing he was dead, that I let him down.

"Are you freaking out?" Nox asks, wiping the back of his hand across his greasy lips. Somehow that's more endearing than it should be.

The innocent way he's looking at me reminds me he's only twenty-two. He's just a kid.

"A little bit," I admit with a laugh before shoving a few fries into my mouth.

"It doesn't change anything. I promise I won't tell anyone anything you've told me."

I shake my head and put my hand up to stop him.

"Oh, god, Nox that's not the problem. I trust you. I'm just trying to get my head around the fact that I've been fucking heartbroken over the past year thinking I failed you like I failed Johnny."

Nox's face falls for a moment before he recovers with a fake smile.

"Mind if I ask you a question?" Nox asks.

"Of course."

"I'm not judging or anything, because I'm a firm believer that everyone's journey is their own but, why aren't you out?"

"I mentioned Johnny to you but I never gave you the details. He was four years younger than me, and kind of a stereotype," I smile remembering Johnny at six years old parading around the house in a pair of our mother's red pumps and a feather boa. God knows where he even found that. "So, when he came out at fourteen it wasn't a surprise to anyone. Then, Gage came out soon after. I knew I liked girls, but as I entered my middle teen years I couldn't deny the part of me was also attracted to guys. It was confusing for me. In some ways I feel like it might have been easier to just be gay because at least then it would've been cut and dry. For a short period of time I had myself convinced my attraction to guys was just a weird phase because the two people closest to me were gay. And then Johnny started getting picked on at school and I thought it would be easier to keep that part of myself a secret. After all, I liked girls a hell of a lot so I didn't think I'd feel like I was missing anything if I never explored that other side of my sexuality." I pause, getting up the nerve for the next part.

"What happened to Johnny?" Nox asks, putting a hand over mine, seeming to sense my turmoil.

"He overdosed on Benzo's which he'd apparently been abusing. We found a huge stash of them in his bedroom after he died. And, uh, we think it was on purpose. We found online chats saying he couldn't stand feeling anything anymore and how badly he was being bullied." My voice cracks as my throat tightens on the last words.

Nox's hand on mine gives a gentle, comforting squeeze.

"You don't have to keep going."

"No, the hard part is over," I assure him with a weak smile. "I felt guilty for a long time, like maybe if I'd told him what I was struggling with he wouldn't have felt so alone. Maybe I could've gotten him help if my head wasn't so far up my own ass. By the time I forgave myself for that I was twenty-five and the idea that I'd be okay *never* trying anything with a man was starting to fade. I really wanted to explore that side of myself. But, I still hadn't told my best friend. That's the holding pattern I've been in for four years now. I've felt too guilty about lying to Gage to go out and explore."

"Why don't you just tell him?" Nox asks.

"He'll hate me. He's not over Johnny's death. They were together and Gage loved him so fucking much. He's still not himself. I'm not sure if he'll ever be the same again. If I tell him I've been lying to him all these years it'll kill him."

"So you're *never* going to tell him?" Nox asks, eyebrows raised.

I shrug helplessly and Nox is kind enough to drop the subject.

When Nox and I get back to the apartment Gage is sitting on the couch watching Netflix. When he sees the two of us coming in together his eyebrows pull together in confusion.

"Oh, were you guys hanging out?"

"I was putting some ink on Nox, then we went out to grab a bite to eat."

Gage grunts in acknowledgement before turning his attention back to the television.

"I'm going to sleep," Nox announces awkwardly before shuffling off toward his room.

I stand beside the couch indecisively for several seconds. What I desperately want is to follow Nox to his room and hold him in my arms again. The way he melted against me when I hugged him at the restaurant rattled something inside me.

I can't follow him, though. Firstly, it would be highly inappropriate. He's my employee now. Not to mention, I can't imagine he's in any sort of place to want a relationship, physical or otherwise. And, secondly, how would I explain to Gage why I'm trailing our new roommate around the apartment like a lovesick puppy?

Instead, I plop down on the couch beside Gage and we watch *LA Ink* in silence.

Nox

Heathens Ink is busy most of the day Saturday, back to back with appointments and walk-ins. It feels good to be running around and learning so much.

Around noon Madden catches me between clients.

"Hey, I was wondering if you want to go grab lunch together down the street?"

"Uh...um...yeah, let me check with Adam real quick." I can't believe Madden wants to hang out with me. The only friend I've ever had was Amanda. "Hey, Madden invited me out to lunch. Do I have time for a break?"

Adam smiles.

"Yeah, that's great. Go get to know Madden, have lunch, no rush."

"Great, can I bring you anything back?" I offer, forcing my eyes not to roam over him as he reaches into the cabinet above his computer to grab a roll of paper towels. When his shirt rides up a few inches exposing a half inch of tempting skin I fail miserably.

"Can you bring me a turkey sandwich and fries?" He asks.

"Sure thing. I'll see you in a bit."

When I head back up front Madden is waiting for me, fiddling with his phone and leaning against the front desk.

We head down the street to a small cafe. I remember last night Adam mentioned that Madden is a recovering addict as well. It would be so great to have an accountability person. I've been having a surprisingly easy time since leaving rehab, but I know the time will come when my resolve will be tested.

"So, how are you doing with everything?" Madden gets right to the point once we're seated.

"Surprisingly well."

"Really? Because you don't need to front to me. I don't know if Adam would've mentioned it to you, I may not have track marks I'm still an addict through and through."

"Yeah, he told me last night. No details or anything, just said that he believes in second chances."

Madden nods and smiles.

"Yeah, I owe my life to that man," Madden agrees. I do my best to ignore the niggle of jealousy. "If you want, you can come with to my support group I go to every week. It's not strictly for drug addicts, but a number of people there are. It's always good to have people who understand."

"I'd love to come, thank you."

"Getting settled in at Gage and Adam's place?"

"Yeah…" I trail off, remembering the slightly hostile look I'd received from Gage last night when Adam and I got home. "Can I ask you a question?"

"Of course."

"Gage and Adam...?"

Madden nearly chokes on the water he just took a sip of before setting the glass down on the table and laughing out loud.

"Oh my god, no. What? No, definitely not."

"Why is that so funny?" I bristle. Had no one else noticed the hostile protective vibe Gage had going on when it came to Adam?

"They're like brothers. Plus, Adam is straight. And, I'm almost positive Gage is still in love with Adam's dead brother."

"Oh." I reach for my own glass of water. Obviously I'm not going to correct the 'straight' thing, but the rest of it seems valid enough.

"Oh my god, you have a little crush on Adam, don't you?" Madden teases.

I feel the heat in my cheeks as I cast my gaze around for a waitress to come take our order and interrupt us.

"It's okay, I had a little crush on him when I first started at Heathens, too."

"You did?"

"Well, yeah, it's hard not to. He's got that whole lumbersexual thing going on and he's just such a good person. Plus, how can you *not* crush on a man who's saved your life. As I'm saying that I realize I might have a bit of a savior complex. I'm engaged to a man who rescued me during a mass shooting at a club last year." Madden flashes a silver ring in my direction with pride.

"Holy shit, I remember seeing that on the

news. You were there?"

"Yeah. I took a few bullets and I won't bore you with the details of my recovery but it was quite dramatic. There was a character arch, struggles to face, even a surprising, emotional twist. But I got my Happily Ever After."

I chuckle and decide I think I like Madden. *I did it, I made a new friend.*

"Well, I can't say I have a hero complex, per se, but it would be nice to date a guy who's nice to me for a change," I admit, adding a laugh to keep the comment from coming off as too dark. The pitying look Madden gives me suggests I missed the mark.

"He's out there," Madden assures me.

When we get back to Heathens, Royal is keeping an eye at the front desk chatting with a teenage boy.

"Hey Nox, I want you to meet Liam. He hangs out here a lot so don't mind him," Royal introduces me to the boy. "He's my son."

My mouth falls open at the declaration before I can try to school my features. It doesn't seem like there's more than seven years between them, how can Royal be his dad?

"Oh my god, Royal, you're so embarrassing," Liam rolls his eyes in true teenager fashion. "He's my brother, my legal guardian, and a total idiot."

I laugh and shake my head as Royal and Liam argue back and forth.

I stretch my arms over my head, working a kink out of my back and suddenly Liam and Royal are silent. I glance down and realize my shirt pulled up and exposed the extensive scarring on my lower abdomen. I feel heat creeping into my cheeks as I tug my shirt back down.

"That looks rough, your dick didn't get burned off did it? That would suck," Royal jokes.

I open my mouth to tell him that, thank god, my dick is perfectly fine. But Liam spins on Royal and socks him in the shoulder.

"Dude, that is so fucking rude. You don't just go around asking random people about their genitals."

Royal's smile falls and he shoots me an apologetic look.

"Sorry."

"It's okay. And, my dick is just fine, thanks for your concern," I deadpan.

Owen walks through the front door and Liam's eyes bug out of his head before he plasters on a bored expression.

"Hey, Owen," Liam greets him with a nod before casting his gaze down and fiddling with his t-shirt.

"Hey, man," Owen greets with a smile, holding up his fist for a bump as he passes. "You got some new photography to show me?"

"Uh, yeah," Liam says, smiling and nodding.

The way he's looking at Owen like he invented oxygen is kind of adorable.

Royal clears his throat and then shoots Liam a warning glance.

"I'm going to find Adam and see what he's got planned for me for the rest of the day," I say, sensing unresolved family issues.

Adam

There's a light rap at my door and I call out for whoever is there to come in.

"Hey, I've got your sandwich," Nox says holding up a takeout box. "I also brought you a chocolate chip cookie."

"Oh man, you've discovered my Kryptonite." I wave him in and reach for the food he's got for me.

"Always good knowledge to have," Nox teases.

As he passes me the food our fingers brush and a small thrill goes through me. Little does he know, he might be another of my weaknesses.

"What's red and bad for your teeth?" I set up an anti-joke I saw earlier, remembering how Phoenix and I used to trade morbid humor and terrible jokes over chat.

"What?"

"A brick."

"Oh my god, that joke is the worst," Nox complains but laughs anyway.

There's something about his laugh that does

funny things to my chest.

"Alright funny guy, why don't you tell me a joke?"

"What's red and smells like blue paint?" Nox asks.

"What?"

"Red paint."

"And you think *my* jokes are bad?" I shake my head in mock disappointment.

The afternoon flies by as quickly as the morning had with a combination of appointments and walk-ins filling up my schedule all the way until closing time.

While Nox and I clean up my workspace Gage pops his head in.

"Hey, I'm going to be heading over to Rainbow House tonight, won't be home 'til late."

"Okay, tell everyone I say hi and that I'll do my best to stop by soon."

"Is Rainbow House a bar or something?" Nox asks once Gage is gone.

"No, it's a halfway house for LGBTQ teens who don't have anywhere to go."

Nox's lips part on a quiet gasp and his eyes glaze over slightly.

"That's so amazing. You volunteer to help homeless LGBTQ teens?"

"It's no big deal," I shrug off the awe in his

voice. I love working with the kids down at R.H., but it's not enough. Nothing will ever be enough.

"It *is* a big deal. You are like a real-life superhero," Nox insists.

I feel myself blush and wave off his praise.

"I'm no superhero," I argue. "I'm just doing what I can so no one has to feel as helpless and alone as Johnny did."

"I'm going to have to think of a superhero name for you," Nox carries on as though he didn't hear my protest. "Hmm, let's see...what about lumberjack man?"

"What? That's terrible, what would my super power even be?"

"The ability to chop wood super-fast."

"I feel like there's a sexual innuendo in there somewhere."

Nox barks out a laugh.

"I'd love to go help out at Rainbow House sometime," Nox says casually, but his expression is anything but. I can tell it would mean a lot to him to help some kids who are in a position he's familiar with.

"Do you mind my asking how you ended up on the streets? Were your parents dicks about the gay thing or what?"

"It's kind of embarrassing."

"You don't have to tell me if you're uncomfortable. I was being nosey, forget I even asked," I backpedal, realizing what a dick question that was.

"No, it's cool. My mom was a junkie and a prostitute, dad was some John I assume. We were on and off the street my whole life. Mom would get clean for a little while, we'd get an apartment, and I'd think finally, we're like normal people. But, it never lasted long. Six months to a year later she'd be using again. We weren't always homeless, only about a quarter of the time. Then when I was sixteen my mom overdosed. I'd heard enough horror stories about the system to know I had to disappear before I ended up in it. By that point I'd already been...doing what I had to survive so it wasn't all that new. I had a good friend who took care of me, and I learned to get by."

"Wow." I gaze in awe of the small man standing in front of me. At first glance you'd think he's fragile, maybe a little femme, you might wrongly assume he's weak. But fuck if he isn't made of steal.

"What happened to your friend?" I ask, almost afraid to hear the answer. These stories don't tend to end in a Happily Ever After.

"She was murdered," Nox says, his voice cracking on the last word. Then he clears his throat and goes on. "And you know the rest of my sob story. I'm hoping Tobey Maguire will play me in the Lifetime movie adaptation."

"You can do way better than Tobey Maguire. I'd say you're more of a Zac Efron before he got on steroids. Oh, or Joseph Gordon Levitt, he's sexy cute like you are."

Nox laughs again and I realize how forward

I'm being but it's too late to back off now without looking like an idiot.

"I'll take that as a compliment."

"So, uh, what are you feeling for dinner?"

"I'm up for whatever. I vote we just grab some food and watch a good movie."

"That sounds awesome," I agree, trying not to notice that's exactly the perfect scenario I described for Nox as Phoenix when he asked about what a night with my ideal partner would look like.

I strip out of my clothes and dive between my cool sheets. I wrap my arms around my body pillow and hug it close like a lover.

Nox and I had a fun night together, watching Will Ferrell movies and eating a frozen lasagna I made.

I never would've thought that Phoenix would be exactly as he presented himself in real life. Most people put a different persona forward when they're behind a computer screen. But Nox is every bit as funny, surprising, and easy to talk to as Phoenix was.

Even though I shouldn't, I can't stop myself from mentally replacing the pillow in my arms with Nox in my mind, spooned against me in the dark.

My cock stirs as I imagine kissing and licking along the back of Nox's neck while I tease my erection between the cheeks of that perfect bubble butt he has. I wonder if Nox only likes to bottom? Or does he prefer to top? Maybe he's up for either.

A spike of heat goes through me at the thought of Nox dominating me, tying my hands and fucking me like he owns me.

I drag in a ragged breath as lust heats in the pit of my stomach, my cock now fully hard against my pillow.

I roll forward and reach into my nightstand in search of relief from the burning need now coursing through me. My hand lands on my dildo and I grab it along with the bottle of lube I have stashed in there.

Slicking my fingers I reach back and gently tease my hole. My cock pulses against the pillow between my legs as I imagine Nox's fingers stroking me open.

I bite down on my pillow to stifle a moan as I slip a finger inside, prepping myself for my dildo. My mind returns to the fantasy of being handcuffed by Nox, completely at his mercy. Maybe he'd take his time, torturing me until I'm begging for his dick.

I reach for my lube again and coat my dildo.

I close my eyes and picture Nox kneeling between my legs, the head of his cock nudging against my entrance until he's able to ease inside.

I angle my toy correctly and slowly fuck

myself, my mind still stuck on the fantasy of Nox inside me.

I bite down on my tongue in an attempt to keep myself quiet. The need inside me burns brighter.

"Fuck me harder," I tell the Nox in my mind as I impale myself harder, faster.

My free hand wraps around my dripping cock and I jerk myself in time with the thrusts. In my mind Nox looks down on me with a feral hunger.

"I want to feel you come inside me, please."

My whole body tenses as white hot pleasure courses through my veins. Cum splashes forcefully against my abs and chest as I pant and whimper through my orgasm, wishing like hell Nox was here with me.

The afterglow is interrupted by my need to clean up. I grab a rag off my floor and wipe myself off and then wrap it around my dildo before shoving it in my drawer so that I can remember to clean it before I use it again.

CHAPTER 10

Adam

"Do you have any plans tonight?" I ask Nox as we clean up for the night.

Nox laughs.

"What plans would I have? You're literally my only friend."

"That's not true," I argue. "You and Madden are friends, and Gage is going to warm up to you eventually. And don't forget Dani."

"Okay, fair enough. My point stands that I wouldn't have plans you didn't know about."

Something about that statement warms my center. I can almost convince myself I have some sort of claim over Nox. Not in an abusive or controlling way, but like he's mine to care for.

"You up for an adventure with me?"

Nox's eyes spark with excitement before he can school his expression to nonchalance.

"Depends what it is."

"I've waited way too long for my first gay experience. Care to help me out with that?"

Nox's cheeks pink and his eyes go wide. His tongue peeks out as he wets his lips and it's all I can do not to pounce on him. I realize what my words must've sounded like and Nox seems into the idea.

"Um...uh...what...uh?" He stutters out an attempted response.

"I thought we'd hit a gay club. You know, dance, flirt. It'll be fun."

"Oh," Nox's face falls. "Yeah, that sounds fun."

"Great. Do you know what I'm supposed to wear?"

Nox shrugs and then laughs.

"Hell if I know, I've never been either."

"Great, we can both pop our cherries tonight then."

Nox

I just about creamed my pants when I thought Adam was propositioning me. To my surprise a hint of fear accompanied the arousal when I realized I didn't know exactly *what* Adam wanted from me.

Going to a club with Adam wasn't what I thought he was asking for. But I'm flattered he chose me to share this experience. And like I told him, I've never been either. Not a lot of time for clubbing in my life. At least not like this.

When Harrison was wooing me we went to upscale clubs, stayed in the VIP section, and got bottle service. That's not what tonight is about. This is two guys going out to dance and drink, maybe flirt a little.

My stomach drops as it occurs to me Adam meant flirting with *other* guys. That's what makes the most sense. Why would he take me out to a club where there are hundreds of hot guys and only flirt with me? *Oh god, is he going to hook up with someone tonight?* I know he said he's never been with a guy before, but maybe that's what he meant by his first gay experience. He's going to find some cute guy to get on his knees for him.

Bile rises in my throat at the thought. Both at the image of Adam with a man who isn't me, and of Adam behaving like the men I've gone down on. Picturing Adam with a malicious glint in his eye forcing a young, drunk guy to take his cock deeper, gagging him with it until he can't breathe, is enough to make me sick.

"Hey, are you about ready to go?" Adam asks from the other side of my bedroom door.

"Almost," I call out, forcing myself to calm down. Adam doesn't seem like that type of guy. He's sweet and good.

I grab a black t-shirt out of my closet and tug it on before checking myself in the mirror. I don't know what guys normally wear clubbing but I figure I can't go wrong with a t-shirt and jeans that make my ass look great.

I tug open the door and find Adam standing there in a blue button down shirt with the top few buttons undone and the sleeves rolled up to show off his ink. My eyes continue on to his form fitting jeans that are showing off an enticing yet discrete bulge.

"Wow," I breathe.

"Thank you. You look pretty wow yourself."

"Thanks."

"Ready to go?" he asks when I'm unable to do anything other than stand and stare at him.

"Yeah."

I shouldn't be surprised that on a Saturday night the club is packed. Everywhere I look there are half naked men, dancing, groping, flirting. The pheromones are thick in the air. People are here looking to get laid and no one is pretending otherwise.

"Want a drink?" Adam asks, having to shout in my ear so I can hear him over the music.

I nod and follow him toward the bar.

As we wind between sweaty bodies I notice so many men turning their heads, eyes roaming hungrily over Adam. I can't blame them, but it doesn't mean I like it.

"Haven't seen you here before, sexy. What can I get for you?" the bartender asks, eyeing Adam like he's made of chocolate.

"I'll have whatever's on tap. Nox?"

"Water please," I add.

"This is crazy, I didn't expect it to be so crowded," Adam says near my ear.

I shiver at the feeling of his breath against

my neck and inch closer under the guise of making room for people to shove past.

Once we get our drinks we find a slightly less crowded corner so we can people watch for a few minutes and take it all in.

"There are a lot of guys here. Are you looking for someone to hook up with?" *Wow, real subtle, Nox, great job.*

"Nah, just wanted to hang out with you, maybe dance?"

I nod in agreement, all too pleased with the idea of Adam grinding up on me.

Adam chugs down his drink and then sets the empty glass on an abandoned table before grabbing my hand and dragging me toward the dance floor.

I've never danced before but it doesn't look too difficult.

Adam's arms go around me and to my surprise his front presses up against my back. My ass snugged to his hips. It only takes a few seconds for a tell-tale hardness to wedge itself against me and steal my breath.

For a second I forget what we're supposed to be doing until Adam's hands are on my hips, guiding me in time to the pulsing beat of the techno music.

I melt into Adam, letting his movement and the music guide me. I'm hard as steel as his hands wander over my hips and stomach not staying in any one spot for too long. I want to turn around in his arms and lick his skin, taste his salty sweat. I want to suck his lips and taste his tongue. I want to grind our cocks together until our seed mixes, coating our stomachs as we come.

My cock throbs in the confines of my jeans and I have to wrench myself out of Adam's grasp to keep from embarrassing myself right there on the dance floor.

"I need more water," I call out in way of explanation before fleeing from temptation. I need to get a grip. Adam has been nothing but kind and helpful to me, I owe him better than treating him like nothing more than a John.

I reach the bar and flag down the bartender for another bottle of water. While I'm waiting a man sidles up beside me. If I had to describe my type it would be the opposite of this guy. He's beefy and bald with a mustache that seems to be in business for itself. His smile feels creepy and predatory. I try to inch away without being too obvious but he either doesn't notice or doesn't get the subtle hint.

"Hey, baby. Let me buy you a drink."

"No thanks, I'm just drinking water."

"You're at a bar," he points out.

"Yeah, I'm here to dance. Not that I have to explain myself to you."

"You're a mouthy one, aren't you," his eyes light and he reaches out and grabs my arm. When his fingers wrap around my wrist his nose scrunches in distaste. "The fuck, dude?"

He drops my arm and a simultaneous feeling of relief and shame washes over me.

"This guy bothering you?" Adam asks from behind me.

"No. I think I need some air." I'm not sure I say it loud enough for Adam to hear me but I don't wait to find out. The club is suddenly too crowded, it's stifling.

As soon as I'm outside I take a deep breath, willing my frantic heart to calm down. That was way too many emotions to experience in such a short period, especially for someone who's spent their life numbing emotions with dope.

"Nox," Adam calls my name as he steps out of the club, looking around until his gaze lands on me, leaning against the side of the building.

"Hey, you didn't need to come after me. I needed a second but I was going to come back."

"Did that guy hurt you?" Adam asked, his expression thunderous.

"No. He grabbed my arm but he didn't hurt me," I assure him.

"Then what's wrong?"

My throat tightens and I look down at my scarred arms.

"I'm hideous. No one is ever going to want me like this," I admit my fear, eyes remaining downcast. I can't look at Adam while I throw this pity party. I'm self-conscious enough as it is.

Adam steps into my personal space and forces my face up so I can't avoid his gaze. He trails his index finger down my arm, carefully caressing every inch of marred skin.

"You are perfect. Anyone would be lucky to be with you, to touch you."

A shiver of pleasure runs up my spine at his gentle touch and kind words. Surely he's just being nice. He can't mean that *he* would want to touch me. Not like I want him to anyway.

"Why are you so nice to me?"

"Because…" Adam looks like he's struggling to explain.

"Because I remind you of Johnny?" I ask in a shaky voice.

Adam looks stricken like he's had bucket of water dumped on him. He pulls back his touch and takes a step away to give me space.

"Yeah, because of Johnny," he agrees. "Do you want to dance some more or are you ready to call it a night?"

"I'm kind of tired."

Adam nods in understanding and tilts his head toward the parking lot. I push off the wall and follow him, trying not to let my disappointment suffocate me.

CHAPTER 11

Nox

I'm uploading some pictures of tattoos done over the past few days to the shop's Facebook page when the bell over the door chimes. I look up and paste on a smile as a gorgeous woman with long, dark hair approaches the counter.

"Welcome to Heathens Ink, what can I help you with today?"

She looks me up and down, clearly sizing me up, before giving me a patronizing smile.

"Oh, sweetie, you must be new. I'm here for Adam."

A twinge of jealousy hits me in the stomach. Adam clearly isn't wanting for romantic company, not that I blame him, but it's further proof I need to get over my stupid crush. I don't have a snowball's chance in hell with a guy like him.

"Kira?" Adam approaches from the back of the shop with a mixture of confusion and irritation on his face.

Kira runs toward him and launches herself into his sturdy arms. Meanwhile, I do my best to resist the urge to rip her hair out. He catches her easily, seeing as how she probably weighs about a hundred pounds soaking wet, but still doesn't look entirely thrilled to see her. She whispers something in his ear and he sets her down and leads her back to his office.

I'm not sure how long I stare after them with a pit of dread in my stomach before Dani approaches the front desk humming the Wicked Witch's theme song from the *Wizard of Oz.*

"Can I take that to mean you're not a fan of Kira?" I ask.

"God no, she's a cunt."

I sputter a laugh at Dani's proclamation.

"Is she...Adam's girlfriend?"

"More like fuck buddy. She's got this on again, off again boyfriend and whenever they're off again she comes crawling after Adam like a love-sick puppy. Haven't seen her in ages though. I thought they were finally over for good."

Her explanation does little to ease the jealous rage boiling inside of me.

"She's so pathetic, practically begging Adam to be her boyfriend. Plus, she's a total bitch. Whenever they're fooling around she comes in here and treats us all like shit. And on top of that she's an unscrupulous psycho. She faked a pregnancy once when he was trying to break things off with her. Can you believe that?"

"Jesus, that's insane."

"Please tell me I didn't just hear Kira's voice out here?" Royal asks, peeking out of his workspace.

"Unfortunately, you did."

"I don't get what he sees in her," Dani shakes her head looking back toward Adam's office with a disgusted look on her face.

"Yeah, I thought he was..." Royal trails off, casting a quick glance in my direction.

Does he know about Adam's sexuality?

Adam

As soon as we're in my office I spin on Kira, my jaw clenched and muscles taut.

"What do you want, Kira?"

"You, obviously," she answers, crowding into my personal space and running her hand along my chest. I grab Kira's wrist in a harsh motion that makes her gasp.

"I told you a fucking *year* ago it was *over*. We don't work on any level, go back to your boyfriend." I let go of her wrist, and nod toward the door. "We're done here."

Kira's pouty lips are parted in outrage. In the past it's exactly the kind of expression that would've tempted me to bend her over my desk and fuck her until neither of us could walk right later. This time, though, my cock doesn't so much as stir in interest.

"Is this because of the cute little twink you've got working up front now?" Kira asks with a knowing spark in her vicious eyes.

"What the fuck does that mean?"

"Come on, Adam. We've been fucking for

113

years, you think I couldn't figure out you swing both ways? You have your own dildo for god sake. You realize straight guys don't usually like dildo's up the ass, right?"

"First, that's the stupidest thing I've ever heard. Guys have prostates whether they're gay or straight, so that shit feels awesome regardless. Secondly, I don't get why you're brandying this information around like it's some sort of weapon."

"Because, I also know you don't want Gage to know."

My breath catches and I'm certain the color is draining from my face if Kira's triumphant smile is anything to go by.

"You don't know shit. Get the fuck outta here and don't come back," I spit before opening the door and fixing her with a menacing glare.

Her scowl tells me this isn't over, but she stomps out without any further argument.

I give myself a minute to tamper my anger down before I head back up front.

"Please tell me Kira isn't back," Dani says the second I reach the gaggle of my employees congregated around the front desk.

"I can assure you from the bottom of my heart that Kira is *not* back."

"She was kind of hot," Owen notes casually.

He's only been at Heathens a few months and it's been taking him longer than I'd hoped to settle in and make friends with everyone. I don't know his whole story other than that he was in prison. He seems like a good person so I'm not worried about what he did to land himself there. I just hope he's finding his way in life now that he's out. I make a mental note to do a better job getting Owen involved with everyone here.

"She's literally insane," Dani argues.

"Crazy girls are the best in bed," Owen points out. "Strangely, insane guys are not that great in bed. Weird dichotomy."

A small spike of jealousy jolts through me. It must be nice for Owen to feel so comfortable with his bisexuality.

I notice Nox is quiet, still sitting in front of the computer.

"How's it going with those pictures?" I check with him, noticing his pinched expression.

"It's going great. Just about finished," he glances over and forces a smile.

My hand twitches with the urge to reach over and touch him. Not in a sexual way, just to connect with him.

"Okay, cool. Do you want to come to Rainbow House with me tonight?"

Nox smiles and then frowns.

"Oh shoot, I told Madden I would tag along with him to his group thing tonight. Maybe I can come with you tonight and go with Madden another night."

"No, go with Madden. We can go to R.H. another time, it's not going anywhere."

Nox

"Is this one of those things where I have to stand up and be like 'My name is Nox and I'm a Heroin addict'?"

"No, it's not Narcotics Anonymous. This is a support group. My therapist, Dr. Marvin, pretty much sits back and lets people share and talk amongst ourselves but he's there to help if needed. Otherwise we are here for each other. Feel free to share if you want to, or offer insight or advice to anyone else who shares. It's casual so don't feel any pressure."

"Okay." I follow Madden into the non-descript brick building.

When we get inside it's more or less what I expected. There are about a dozen people there, milling about and talking, chairs arranged in a circle at the center of the room, and a folding table with cookies and a carafe of coffee on it.

Madden takes me around and gives me a brief introduction to each person. Everyone seems friendly and welcoming which eases my nerves a bit.

After a few minutes of general socializing and drinking cheap coffee everyone starts to move to fill the chairs in the center of the room.

As Madden said, the doctor sits back from the group rather than actively participating. And in a seeming unspoken ritual they start to go around the circle, each person either sharing about their week, feelings, or simply waving their hand and passing to the next person.

When the progression reaches me I consider passing, and the look Madden gives me assures me it's okay if I don't want to speak up on my first night. But something in me wants to share.

"Hi everyone, thanks for letting me join you. I'm Nox, as Madden already told you, and I am a Heroin addict. I don't remember much about the night I almost died. In some ways, calling it that feels a bit dishonest, because I easily could've died any night between the ages of fourteen, and the night my boyfriend set me on fire. The only thing I really remember was the feeling of not giving a shit. I didn't care I was dying. I didn't have anything to live for. No one would've missed me. The world would've been no different without me.

"When I woke up in the hospital two weeks later, I could still remember that feeling but I was determined to change everything. I didn't want to be that person anymore with nothing to live for. I wanted to be someone who would impact the world, or at the very least someone with *one* person who would miss me. I haven't touched drugs since that night and I've taken some very positive steps toward building a life. I'm hopeful and I'm grateful. And...that's about it, so thanks for letting me ramble," I conclude with an awkward laugh.

I feel Madden's hand on my shoulder.

"Thank you for sharing that," Madden says and a murmur of agreement goes through the group before the next person starts to share.

After the group session Madden offers to drive me home, but we're only about a mile away and a walk sounds nice so I decline.

I breathe in the cool spring air, gazing up at the stars as I walk, and an unfamiliar sense of peace washes over me. It's like for the first time in my life I'm on the path I'm meant to be on. Nothing else counts, I've left all that shit behind. *This* is my life and I finally have the chance to be happy.

Another more skeptical part of my brain argues that nothing is this easy. Any day now the rug will be pulled out from under me and I'll be back on the street, with a needle in my arm. Or worse, I'll wake up on my dirty, threadbare mattress and this will all have been a dream.

I shudder at the thought.

Then, that shudder becomes a more prominent sense of unease. I glance over my shoulder, having the distinct impression of being followed, but I don't see anyone behind me. I laugh at myself even as my skin continues to prickle and the hair on my neck stands on end. I'm just freaking myself out, that's the only logical explanation.

To my relief, my apartment building comes into view up ahead. I speed up my pace and laugh at myself once more when I reach the door completely out of breath.

"Hey," I greet Gage awkwardly as I step into the apartment and see him sitting on the couch.

I get the feeling Gage doesn't particularly

want me here, in his apartment with him and Adam. Madden insisted there wasn't romantic jealousy behind it, and maybe he's right, but the hostility remains at a simmer between us.

"You can sit if you want," Gage offers.

"Oh...um," I look between the vacant spot on the couch and the hallway leading to my bedroom.

"Sit, I owe you an apology."

I slink onto the open seat, casting a sideways glance at Gage. It's not that I'm *afraid* of him, more that I know if I fuck things up and Gage completely hates me that won't endear me to Adam.

"Relax man, I don't bite," Gage assures me.

I take a breath and force myself to relax my posture.

"You don't owe me an apology. I get why you wouldn't want some random junkie rooming with you."

"That's not it," Gage argues, turning to face me. "Not exactly anyway. It's more that Adam has this fucking complex about saving drug addicts, like it'll somehow bring back Johnny. But Johnny is gone and no matter how many poor souls Adam rescues, Johnny will *always* be gone."

"I understand." I put a comforting hand on Gage's shoulder. "I'm not trying to replace Johnny in your and Adam's life. If it wasn't for Adam I'm not sure I'd still be alive right now, I owe him everything. I know it won't bring Johnny back but the kindness all of you guys are showing me has changed my life."

Gage pats my hand on his shoulder and gives me a tight smile.

"I'm glad to hear that. I'll try to be less of an asshole from here on out, I promise."

"I appreciate it." I laugh and then settle back on the couch to watch whatever Gage has on. "Can I ask you a question?"

Gage grunts what seems to be agreement.

"Do you have feelings for Adam?"

"What?" Gage pauses the show and turns to look at me like I'm wearing a tinfoil hat. "Like, *feelings* feelings?"

I shrug.

"You seem protective of him."

"He's my best friend and a brother to me. *Feelings* for Adam?" Gage wrinkles his nose at the idea and then shudders. Then he stills and his eyes go wide. "Wait, do *you* have a thing for him?"

"No, of course not," I rush to lie.

"Sorry to break it to you, but you're barking up the wrong tree. Adam is as straight as can be."

"What if he wasn't?"

Gage furrows his brows and then shrugs.

"I guess it would've been cool when we were teenagers if he was gay too, since we were best friends and all. But, he was never weird about me or Johnny being gay."

I'm caught between relief that Gage didn't understand my question, and irritation at myself for almost outing Adam unintentionally. I settle for a smile before turning to face the T.V. again. Gage follows suit and we fall into a comfortable silence.

CHAPTER 12

Adam

After leaving Rainbow House for the night I find a text from Owen.

Owen: up for grabbing a drink?
Me: sure, meet at O'Malley's in fifteen?
Owen: cool

This is the first time Owen has reached out to me to hang out so I'm not sure what to expect. Is he finally getting comfortable and wants to make friends? Is something bothering him and he needs someone to talk to? Or does he just not like drinking alone?

I point my car in the direction of O'Malley's so I can find out.

When I walk in I nod a greeting to the 'hot bartender' as Dani calls him. I believe his actual name is Beau. But with the way he always flirts with customers, both men and women, I doubt he'd object to being called hot bartender either.

Then, I spot Owen sitting on the far end of

the bar nursing a beer.

Owen walked into Heathens six months ago looking for a job. I hadn't particularly been looking for someone at the time but when I led him back to my office I could tell he was nervous. Then, he sat down in the chair I offered, looked me right in the eye, and told me he just got out of prison but the charges were trumped up. He said he was desperate for a second chance and would do anything to prove himself.

I couldn't find it in my heart to turn him away. I can only imagine how difficult it must be to find a job with a criminal conviction on your record. And then he showed me a portfolio of the tattoos he'd done before he was locked up and I couldn't turn him down.

Owen has remained a bit quiet and reserved, but he's brought a raw, unique style to Heathens that sets him apart from the other artists and has a line of clients waiting months for an appointment with him.

"Hey man," I greet him, sliding onto the stool next to his.

"Hey."

It only takes a minute for my favorite beer to appear in front of me with a smile from Beau.

"You seeing anyone, Beau?" I ask, and then blush when he smiles at me.

"Why? Are you interested?"

"Not me, Dani. She's the-"

"I know who she is," Beau assures me. "She's

cute, I'll have to keep that in mind. Things are kind of complicated with my roommate right now, we're in a weird friends with benefits place and I'm not sure either of us knows where we want it to go from here. Or, rather, where it *should* go. He's a great guy, too good for me...Oh lord, I'm rambling," Beau puts a hand over his mouth and laughs. I hadn't noticed the faint southern lilt to his voice before. I've gotta give it to Dani, she's got good taste.

"Good luck with your roommate," I offer.

"Thanks, darlin'." Beau winks and then saunters away.

"He's hot, too bad Dani's already got dibs," Owen laments, watching Beau's ass as he retreats.

"Yeah," I agree, slightly mesmerized by the sight as well.

When Owen's eyes cut over to me with surprise I realize my mistake.

"Oh, shit." I close my eyes and take a deep gulp of my beer.

"I suspected, but I wasn't sure."

"You suspected? Damn, maybe I'm worse at hiding it than I thought. First Kira, then Royal, now you. Maybe Gage already knows, too."

"Nah, Gage is oblivious," Owen assures me. "Why are you hiding, anyway?"

"It's complicated. Suffice to say Gage will hate me because I kept it a secret too long so now I can't see a way out without losing my best friend."

"Life's too short not to experience," Owen

says wisely.

"Believe me, I know about how short life is."

My mind goes immediately to Johnny and all the things he'll never get to experience. Would he and Gage have gotten married one day? Had a few kids? What career would he have chosen? What kind of a man would Johnny have grown to be?

All these unanswered questions because he chose to take his life instead of talk to one of us. A familiar anger simmers in the pit of my stomach, followed by guilt for feeling anything but love for my dead brother.

"So, not that I'm complaining, but is this just a social hang out or should I be worried about you?" I ask.

"Social," Owen shrugs. "I've been stand-offish since I've started at Heathens and that needs to change. I like working for you, and I like everyone at the shop. I'm going to start making more of an effort."

"That's awesome, I'm glad to hear that."

"Now, back to the more interesting subject at hand, are you and Nox hooking-up then or what?"

"What? Where did you even get that idea?"

"He looks at you like you're his savior. He's got it bad for you."

"Wouldn't it be skeevy for me to fool around with an employee?"

"That depends."

"On?"

"Whether the employee *wants* to fool around with you," Owen says with a laugh.

"We knew each other before," I admit.

"You did?"

"Yeah, we used to talk online. I didn't know it when I hired him, he told me a few days later. We always got along so well online, I felt like he really *got* me."

"You've convinced me, you absolutely have to go for it. It's too perfect to pass up," Owen insists.

"You think?"

"I think," Owen mocks. "Go for it or you might end up regretting it."

"I'll consider it, thanks man. So, we've dug into my love life, what about yours?"

"Not much going on," Owen shrugs. "I don't feel like it's the right time for me right now. I need a few years to play the field. Believe it or not I'm a big believer in fate and intuition. When the time is right, the person for me will be there."

"That is surprisingly zen for an ex-con."

"Hey, you don't even know what I was in prison for. Maybe I started some hippie cult," he challenges.

"Did you?"

"No."

We both laugh and I feel extremely glad Owen decided to reach out to me tonight. This was exactly what I needed and I think Owen is going to become a great friend.

When I get home a few hours later Nox is sitting on the couch in the dark watching something on the television.

"Hey," I whisper in case Gage is asleep.

Nox startles and screeches, clutching his chest like an old lady having a heart attack.

"Jesus fuck, you scared the hell out of me."

"I'm sorry," I cover my mouth to suppress my laugh.

"I'm watching some movie on Netflix where this deaf chick doesn't know there's a dude in her house, then you sneak up on me like that. I nearly peed myself."

I plop down on the couch beside him, Owen's words ringing in my ears.

"You should've seen your face when I scared you," I tease, mimicking his terrified expression for comedic effect.

Nox punches my shoulder and laughs.

"Shut up, you would've been scared, too."

Nox

The air in the room seems to shift as our laughter fades. I look over at Adam and find him looking back.

His eyes flick over my face like he's searching for something and the crease between his brows makes me wonder what he's thinking so hard about. I wonder for the millionth time how he kisses, what his lips taste like. I've never been this obsessed with kissing before but my brain is like a broken record lately.

Subconsciously, I feel myself leaning forward, and to my surprise, Adam is leaning forward too.

Our mutual approach is slow and measured, like we're both afraid to scare the other off if we move too fast.

His breath smells like chocolate as it bathes my face and my hands start to tremble. I mentally send out a prayer to every deity I can think of not to let Adam come to his senses until *after* I get the chance to kiss him and know what it feels like for just a few seconds.

When his lips finally ghost against mine it's like an electric jolt to every nerve ending. Then, he lets out a defeated sound and crushes his lips against mine and my heart nearly explodes out of my chest.

The kiss is sweet and exploratory as his tongue sweeps against my lips, seeking access. I open to him without hesitation, looping my arms around the back of his neck and pulling myself flush against him.

My skin feels like it's the only thing keeping me from bursting into a million beams of light.

Adam's hands gently roam my body. Not harsh and demanding like I'm used to, but reverently. Each breathy sound that falls from his lips between kisses burrows into my heart to make a permanent home.

Adam pulls his lips from mine and I whimper in protest. He presses his forehead against mine as we both attempt to catch our breath.

"I'm so sorry. God that was so inappropriate," Adam laments in a pained tone.

"No." I clutch desperately at the front of his shirt, unwilling to let him pull away. "Please, don't tell me that the best moment of my life was a mistake."

"You're my employee, and you're going through so much," Adam argues weakly.

"I don't care. Please, Adam, give it a chance. Give *us* a chance?" I don't know what's making me so bold, but now that I've had a taste of what it can feel like to have someone care about you, I can't let it go, not without a fight.

"Okay," Adam breathes after a second and I nearly cry in relief before scrambling into his lap and kissing him again.

More confident now, my tongue sweeps along the inside of Adam's hot mouth. His hands grip my hips and then wander up my back, underneath my shirt. I shiver at the contact of his rough fingers against my skin.

As our kissing drags on with no attempt on Adam's part to get my clothes off I start to feel out of my depth. I don't think he's been with a guy before so am I supposed to let him set the pace? Or, is he assuming I'll lead? Then something else occurs to me...it's only fair for me to tell Adam the full extent of my past before he makes the decision to be in a sexual relationship with me.

I force myself to end the kiss and lean back on his lap.

"Can we talk for a minute?" I ask, putting my hands on his pecs and then running them slowly up to his shoulders before bringing them up to rub his neck. He gives an appreciative moan at the impromptu massage and tilts into my touch like a cat being pet.

"Of course we can talk. You'd better stop that before you put me to sleep, though."

Adam's hands slide down to my waist and his thumbs start to trace rhythmic circles against the skin of my hips.

"The thing is...I used to, um, do *things* for money." I bite down on my bottom lip as soon as the words are out, heart thundering as I wait for Adam's reaction.

His eyes fill with pity and concern.

"I kind of figured," he admits.

"I was tested for STD's in the hospital after..." I gesture to the scars on my arms instead of saying the words out loud. "And I haven't been with anyone or shot up since then, so I'm safe and everything. I mean, obviously we should still use condoms. If you even *want* to fool around with me, of course."

Adam cuts off my rambling with a quick

press of his lips to mine.

"I want you, Nox. I would've thought that was pretty obvious," he teases, pressing his hips up against me so I can feel his erection against my ass. "We don't need to rush anything. You might've guessed that I haven't been with a guy before but that doesn't mean I want to jump straight into bed. Can I take you on a date?"

"You want to *date* me?" My stomach flutters. No one has wanted to date me before. Sure, Harrison took me out to fancy dinners and stuff but that wasn't the same. That was to soften me up so he could use me. I'd spent a lot of time discussing abusive relationships with my therapist in rehab.

"Yeah, if that's okay with you."

"It's okay with me," I feel a smile spreading across my lips as I look at Adam with a sudden shyness. Is it possible this is real? Can a man like Adam really want a man like me? "It has to be a secret, doesn't it?" I ask, realizing what the catch is.

"For now. I'm sorry. Is that okay?"

I think about it for a few seconds. I don't *love* the idea of having to sneak around with Adam. But it's not something I can't live with.

"It's okay," I assure him.

"Tomorrow, I'll take you on our first date."

"You're kind of sweet, has anyone ever told you that?"

"No and you'd better not go spreading that around. I have a reputation to uphold as rugged and masculine."

"Your secret's safe with me," I assure him with feigned solemnity.

Adam pinches my side and I giggle, attempting to wiggle out of his grasp. But Adam wraps his arms around me and covers my lips with his once again. My heart flutters and flips at the playful way he teases and nips at my mouth.

"Are you sure you need to take me on a date first?" I tease, circling my hips to grind my ass against the distinct bulge he's sporting.

Adam groans quietly and cants his hips up against me.

"Yes, I need to take you on a date first because you deserve it. You're not just a place to stick my dick, you're a person who's important to me. I want to do this right."

My throat tightens and my eyes feel a little misty. Unable to form words, I wrap my arms around Adam's neck and pull him in for the tightest hug I can muster.

His arms are strong around my waist as he returns the hug, his hot breath tickling my neck, his touch filling my entire body with a peaceful warmth I've never felt before.

"I should go to bed," I say, pulling away reluctantly.

"Okay. Sleep well." Adam kisses his index finger and then pressing it to my lips.

My heart gives a little flutter at the adorable gesture from a man who seems so outwardly gruff.

"Dream of me?" I ask hopefully.

"Count on it, Bird."

"Bird?" I ask, cocking my head to the side.

"You are the phoenix. You're a bird born out of fire, never destroyed, only ever becoming stronger."

"You are way too charming, it's dangerous," I accuse, narrowing my eyes with playful suspicion. "Good night."

I hop off his lap and head for my bedroom before I can change my mind.

CHAPTER 13

Adam

A loud, jaw-cracking yawn erupts from me as I stare at the damn financial spreadsheets taunting me.

It's difficult to focus on my numbers on the best of days but today I'm running on no sleep and am distracted by the date I'm taking Nox on tonight.

A date I have yet to plan. I don't want to be predictable, especially since Nox has never gone on a date before. I want to do something special for him. I want to give him a night to remember.

I groan and rub my face. Since when am I so sappy? One minute I was determined not to give into this little crush, the next I had my tongue down his throat, dry humping him like my life depended on it.

My cock perks up at the memory.

Nox is too fragile to be someone I use for experimentation. With that in mind, maybe I'm making a huge mistake taking him on a date to begin with. There's no way he's in a position to be looking to date. He got out of an abusive relationship and then a drug addiction less than a year ago.

I stand up and stretch, my muscles protesting after spending the last two hours hunched over my computer.

A light knock comes at my door.

"Come in," I call out.

The door creaks open and Nox peeks his head in. His dark hair is falling into his blue eyes, shining as he smiles.

"Hey boss man," Nox says with a teasing lilt. "You taking a break for lunch at all? Or do you want me to bring you something?"

Nox nibbles his bottom lip while he waits for my response, his fingers fidgeting on the hem of his shirt. Why is that so damn endearing?

"I'll tag along with you to grab lunch if that's cool?"

"Of course. Dani's coming, too," Nox adds.

I ignore the pang in my chest. I kind of wanted him all to myself. Now I'm getting greedy. I can have him all to myself tonight. And just like that, all doubts about whether dating him is a good idea are all blown out of the water. Good idea or not, I can't resist the pull I feel toward him.

And the way Nox is smiling as I gather myself to leave the shop for a little bit, I think he feels the pull, too.

When I get up front Nox and Dani are laughing about something and for a second I pause and drink in the happiness oozing from every pore in Nox's body. It's like he's made of sunbeams and I don't understand how someone who's been through everything he's been through can be so positive and so strong. He called *me* a superhero? He's crazy. If anyone around here has superpowers it's Nox.

"You guys ready to go?" I ask.

"Yeah," Dani grabs the sign from under the desk that says 'Please yodel for service' and we head out.

"Oh, Dani I almost forgot to tell you, Beau thinks you're cute but he's also in a complicated situation with his roommate so it seems like you've got a fifty-fifty shot with him."

Dani's mouth falls open and then she first pumps and starts to do a little dance right there on the sidewalk.

"I wonder if his roommate is hot too. I might be able to work that to my advantage," Dani jokes. "Wait, how do you know all this?"

"I was at O'Malley's last night with Owen and I told him you had a little crush on him."

"Oh my god! That's so embarrassing, jerk."

"Hey, you were loving me two seconds ago."

Dani grumbles at me and I laugh.

"You were out with Owen last night?" Nox asks in a would-be casual voice.

I'm about to tease him about being jealous when I remember Dani is with us.

"Yeah, Owen texted me to grab a drink after I left Rainbow House. We talked and he gave me some great advice about living in the moment and going for it when I want something."

Nox gives me a knowing smile.

"Sounds like good advice."

"You guys are being weird," Dani accuses, eyeing us with suspicion.

"No, we're not. You're delusional from hunger. Let's pick up the pace so we can get some food for you."

She's obviously unconvinced but doesn't push the subject.

After lunch, I set Nox up to shadow Royal on some ink for the afternoon and go in search of Owen for some advice.

"Hey, got a minute?" I ask, poking my head into Owen's work space.

I notice he's got a few photographs of Liam's hanging up on his walls and he's currently working on a sketch.

"Of course, what's up?"

I step in and quietly close the door behind me.

"I took your advice last night."

Owen looks perplexed for a minute before a smile breaks out on his face.

"No shit?" He asks. "You hooked-up with Nox?"

"Not exactly. We kissed and I asked if I could take him on a date tonight."

Owen's smile softens.

"Aw, you like him, don't you?"

"I don't know, he feels special somehow. I think it's because we got to know each other so well last year online and now he's here and he's so much more than I imagined."

"Yeah, you've got it bad," Owen repeats with a laugh. "That's great, I'm happy for you."

"Thanks. But now I have no idea what to do. Where do I take him on a date? How do you act on a date with a guy? I'm so out of my element right now."

"Relax, going on a date with a guy is no different than a girl."

"I've never gone on a date with someone I cared about. He's never been treated nicely, I want to show him a good time. I want to make sure he feels special."

"The fact that you care this much about him having a good time is a good start. Don't stress too much. Just think about something you think he'd enjoy. You don't need to get too fancy, just let him know it means this much to you."

"Okay, thanks man."

Nox

My stomach flutters and flips as I glance at the clock and realize it's almost time to close up shop for the day. I've spent the last eighteen hours vacillating between feeling so giddy I can barely keep from giggling to worrying Adam will have changed his mind about the whole thing before our date happens.

"You're more fidgety than a squirrel on crack. What's up with you?" Dani asks, eyeing me with suspicion.

I chuckle at her analogy.

"Nothing," I lie.

"Yeah, I'm not buying that."

"I can't tell you," I say apologetically, biting my bottom lip and giving her a pleading look. I'm so bad at lying and if she pushes it I'm sure my face will give me away in a second.

"Ooo a secret, how intriguing. Can't you give me a tiny hint so I can live vicariously through you? My life is so boring," Dani pouts.

"Maybe you should see about being the meat in that bartender-roommate sandwich to spice up your life instead of being nosy," I suggest with a cheeky grin.

"Believe me, I'm strategizing."

"Good luck and godspeed," I say with mock solemnity.

"Ready to head out?" Adam asks, appearing from the hallway.

I fight against the overly enthusiastic response threatening to burst from me and settle for a quick nod.

"See you tomorrow, Dani," I give her a quick kiss on the cheek before turning to follow Adam out.

I'm quiet as we make our way to Adam's car, afraid to ask if our date is still on for tonight in case the answer is no.

"So, um, Gage is working for a few more hours so we don't have to sneak out or anything. That is if you're still up for a date tonight?"

"Yes," I answer too quickly.

Adam chuckles and then turns to face me. He glances around before pushing me up against his car and covering my mouth with his. I let out a little whimper as his tongue shoves its way past my lips and I clutch his shirt to steady myself.

A burst of heat seers through my veins as I return the kiss with equal fervor.

When Adam pulls away I'm left lightheaded and scrambling to keep my mental footing.

"Let's go home and get ready for our date," Adam suggests.

I nod, unable to form words in my mushy brain.

The sound of the shower running is seriously distracting me from the task of getting ready for my date. Or maybe it's the image of Adam all naked and soapy that's so distracting.

I rummage through my dresser trying to find something adequate. It would help if I knew what Adam has in mind for tonight.

My eyes flick to my bed and my mind starts to spin over the after date scenario. What does he expect for that portion of the evening? My stomach tightens in an unpleasant way as the filthy, unworthy feelings wash over me. Men using me. Men hurting me.

I take a deep breath trying to calm my nerves. My mind returns to the gentle way Adam's hands explored me last night, never forceful or demanding. He would never hurt me or use me. Right?

A knock on my door startles me.

"I realized I didn't give you any hint about how to dress. Wear something warm," Adam calls through the door.

"Okay," I call back.

There's silence for a minute and I assume Adam has moved on to his room, but then he speaks again.

"I'm excited about our date," he says.

My heart swells in my chest and warm tingles spread through my limbs. *No, Adam would never hurt me.*

"Me too," I manage to force the words past the lump in my throat.

A few seconds later I hear Adam's door closing and I force myself to get my ass in gear so I can be ready to go when Adam is.

I pull on a pair of dark wash jeans and tug a tee-shirt over my head followed by a hoodie since Adam said to dress warm. Not exactly as fancy as I'd hoped to be on my first date, but warm at least.

When I step out of my bedroom, I startle to find Adam waiting.

"Jeez, I'm gonna have to put a bell on you or something before you give me a heart attack."

Adam laughs, shoving his hands in his pockets and shifting his weight on his feet. His eyes roam over me like he can't believe I'm standing there. I self-consciously tug at the hem of my hoodie worried that I underdressed.

"Is this okay?" I ask, looking down at my outfit, suddenly second guessing myself.

"Yeah, it's perfect." Adam licks his lips, eyes flicking over my body and then settling on my lips. "Ready to go?"

I nod, biting my bottom lip against a smile that will surely give away just how excited I am.

This is nice, but I need to keep it in perspective. Adam is looking to explore a new side to his sexuality and he's a good man so he's going to be nice and polite, take me out, and treat me well. That's already more than I'm used to and probably more than I deserve. So I'm not going to ruin it by making it into more than it's meant to be. I'm going to enjoy Adam's attention and affection while it lasts and when he moves on I'm going to be okay with it.

Adam holds his hand out to me and I take it, trying to ignore the tingle that runs up my arm at the contact.

When we get outside to his car Adam opens the door for me and I melt a little.

"You know, you don't have to do all this."

"Why wouldn't I?" Adam asks.

"I'm only-" Adam cuts me off with a quick kiss.

"You're amazing. You're a fighter. You, Lennox Dalton are my hero."

"Shut up, we've already decided that if anyone is a hero it's you," I argue, trying to hide the burning behind my eyes.

"You can be the hero, and I'll be your sidekick," Adam suggests.

"I'll consider it."

I climb into the car and notice a few shopping bags in the back seat I hadn't seen earlier.

"What do you have back there?" I ask.

"Supplies," Adam answers, sliding into the driver seat.

My mind immediately goes to the gutter. There's half a dozen bags back there so it has to be more than just condoms and lube. What other supplies can he think we need? Too afraid to ask, I settle into my seat and try not to worry too much about it.

We ride in comfortable silence for the next few minutes, the radio playing quietly in the background as I watch the city fly by outside the window.

"It's weird, you wouldn't think it would be that different than Chicago, I mean steel buildings are steel buildings, right? But there's a totally different vibe here. Or maybe I'm different here," I muse.

The warmth of Adam's hand lands on my

thigh in a comforting way.

"I wasn't kidding before, you amaze me."

"There's nothing amazing about me," I argue. "I just didn't want to die, and I was dying every day. I'm not sure if I've ever really lived before. I've certainly never lived the way I did when you kissed me."

"I could say the same." Adam moves his hand up from my thigh to clasp my hand and my stomach flutters.

"Are you going to tell me where we're going?" I finally brave the question. "Or, what kind of *supplies* we need that fill six bags?"

Adam chuckles, not taking his eyes off the road.

"We're almost there, you'll see soon."

It's not long before we pull up in front of a brick building in a less populated part of town.

"Where are we?"

"Rainbow House," Adam answers with a smirk.

"Oh, yay! Is this our date?" I bounce in my seat. The minute Adam mentioned this place the other day I knew I had to come here, and likely make coming here a regular thing. The fact that he made this our first date instead of throwing away money on a dumb movie makes me like him even more.

"It is," Adam confirms. "You can look in the bags if you want."

I unbuckle and twist in my seat, reaching for

the bags in the backseat. I peer into the first one to find several bags of jumbo marshmallows. The next bag contains grahm crackers. And a third is filled with chocolate bars.

"I don't get it."

"There's an empty lot behind the shelter. We're going to build a bonfire with the kids and make s'mores."

"Make what?" I ask, cocking my head.

Adam's mouth falls open in horror.

"You've never had s'mores?"

"Uh, no?"

"You build a campfire then you make roasted marshmallows, put on a graham cracker and chocolate sandwich and you're in business. It's heaven."

"Oh, well, FYI there aren't a lot of campfire treats for kids of junkies," I point out with a laugh.

Adam's face falls for a second.

"This sounds amazing, thank you," I add quickly before I ruin the mood.

"Just wait until you meet the kids," Adam says, perking up again before jumping out of the car and rushing around to open my door for me before I get the chance to do it myself.

"Two days in a row, Adam?" A matronly woman notes when we enter the building.

"I brought my new friend with me. Mary, this is Nox," Adam introduces us.

I hold out a hand to shake but Mary brushes it aside and pulls me into a hug. I tense at first before relaxing into her touch. It's nice. It feels like what a mother's hug *should* feel like. I try to remember for a second if my mother ever hugged me. If she did I don't remember it.

"Please release my new employee, Mary. The kids are going to flip when they see what I've got planned for them tonight."

"Oh hush, this boy needs a good hug, I can tell."

When she finally releases me, I notice a slight dampness to my cheeks. I hurry to wipe it away while giving her a grateful smile.

"Thank you."

Adam shifts uncomfortably beside me. I look over and he's eyeing me with concern.

"This isn't starting out how I pictured. Was this the worst idea for a first date ever?"

"Oh my god, no, this is so perfect I can't stand it. Now let's go make some marshmallow treats with the kids."

I notice Adam putting a little space between us as we head toward a double door off to one side. Then it occurs to me that of course these kids can't know about me and Adam. Gage has mentioned coming by here too. Who knows if one of the kids would slip and tell him.

My heart sinks a little but I recover quickly when we step into what seems to be the common room. There are about a dozen kids ranging from young teens to older teens. There seems to be a sort of organized chaos to the group, like a party but all the kids are pretty well behaved. On a couch, off to one side, I spot Royal's brother playing video games with a few other boys. Another group of kids sit around a table playing a card game. And still a few others are sitting in a circle just talking and laughing.

"I thought Liam lived with Royal?"

"He does, he just comes here a lot to hang out. I think it's nice for him to have people his age to relate to."

The emotions welling up inside nearly choke me. Maybe if I'd had a place like this, even to hang out a few hours a couple times a week, who knows how my life could've been different.

"Are you okay?" Adam asks.

"Yeah, I'm just so happy a place like this exists."

"Me too," Adam agrees. "I always wondered if things would've been different for Johnny if he'd known about a place like this and had people he felt he could relate too. Maybe if I'd told him I'm bi. Maybe if a million things had been different..."

I put a hand on Adam's shoulder.

"You didn't let him down."

"How can you know that?" Adam argues.

"Because, it isn't in you to let someone hurt if there's anything you can do about it. Some things are outside our control. You would've helped him if you'd known. It's not your fault."

Adam relaxes into my touch and lets out a shaky breath.

"Thank you."

"Hey, I didn't know you were coming by tonight," Liam calls out to Adam with a smile.

"Yup, just here to spy on and embarrass you. Which of these young men have you been swapping spit with?"

Liam blushes at Adam's teasing and the guys who are playing video games all start ribbing each other about who wants to kiss who.

"Anybody up for a bonfire and some s'mores?" Adam offers loudly, eliciting a burst of excitement throughout the room. "Nox and I are going to get the fire started. Anyone is welcome to join us, but you all better know how to behave appropriately around a bonfire or you'll be in big trouble." Adam's threat is half-hearted but all the kids seem to take him seriously enough.

Adam's hand twitches toward mine and for a second I think he's going to reach for me. But then he shoves his hand in his pocket instead.

Adam

The bonfire roars and the sound of the kids laughing and enjoying the night fills my heart with joy. I glance over at Nox and the unadulterated delight in his face lets me know I made the right choice for our first date.

In the dark with everyone distracted I feel safe enough reaching over and lacing my fingers through Nox's. He looks over at me, eyes wide with surprise, and then settles into a content smile.

"Alright, show me how to make this marshmallow thing."

I laugh and reluctantly release his hand so I can show him how to make a s'more.

"It's all about cooking the marshmallow just right," I explain as I hold a stick over the fire. "Some people lack patience and will shove it right into the flame and burn the shit out of it. But, if you give it time, and rotate it just right, you can have the perfect, golden, melty treat."

I feel Nox's eyes on me and when I turn my head, sure enough, he's looking at me with awe.

"What?" I ask with a nervous chuckle. "Something on my face?"

"No." Nox shakes his head. Even in the fire light I can see the pink in his cheeks as he bites down on his bottom lip and his expression turns shy. "I just can't believe I'm here with you."

"Why's that?"

"I had such a crush on you when we were chatting online. You were so nice to me and endearing in the way you can't tell a good joke to save your life."

"Excuse you, I tell amazing jokes."

"Nope, your jokes are truly awful."

"Shut up and take your marshmallow."

Nox laughs and holds up the graham cracker and chocolate so I can deposit the marshmallow. I watch as he bites into it, waiting for his verdict. His eyes light up.

"Sweet lord this is delicious."

"Told you," I gloat. "It's because I made you a perfectly cooked marshmallow."

"I'm sure," Nox rolls his eyes and laughs. He finishes the s'more and my eyes fall to a fleck of marshmallow on his bottom lip. I want to lean in and lick it off. I glance around and find no one paying attention to us. *Fuck it.* I go for it, leaning in and swiping my tongue along his bottom lip, groaning quietly at the delicious, sweet taste I find there.

When I pull back I catch Liam eyeing me with surprised interest.

Damn. Busted.

I decide to worry about it later. Right now all I want to do is enjoy my date with Nox and forget about the stupid closet I'm still locked in.

CHAPTER 14

Adam

When we enter the apartment, I let out a relieved breath to find it empty. I'd been strategizing the entire ride home about how to sneak Nox into my room without Gage noticing. I'd come up with the ruse of pretending to want to show Nox something on my desktop computer. Lame, but it would have sufficed.

Luckily, I don't have to lie to my best friend's face. Instead I'm able to simply turn to Nox and tilt his face up so I can kiss him. His lips are warm and pliable under mine.

"I don't want our date to end," Nox complains against my mouth.

"You could come to my room. We could close your door so Gage would assume you're asleep in there, and you could stay the night in my bed," I suggest.

Nox tenses for a second before nodding.

"Trust me?"

"With my life," Nox whispers.

A shiver runs through my body before I grab Nox's hand and lead him down the hall to my room.

I'm all for taking things slow, but as soon as the door is closed Nox pounces on me. His mouth is hot and demanding, his lips still taste like marshmallows and chocolate.

Every cell in my body is crying out for Nox. Our hands grasp and fumble in an attempt to undress each other, like if we can't be naked together in the next thirty seconds we'll die.

The pace at which we lose our clothes could probably set a land speed record.

Nox's eyes roam over my body, and when they land on my abdomen they widen. He reaches out with a trembling hand and I look down to see what he's so fascinated by. His fingers brush a tattoo I got last year when we were talking online. I forgot for a second that I even had it.

"From ashes we rise," Nox murmurs, tracing each word with a trembling finger. "When?"

"Last year. Even when I only knew you through a screen there was something about you I couldn't shake. I wanted to save you from yourself, but it was more than that. I was so drawn to you but I was also afraid of what would happen if I couldn't convince you to come here. When you told me these words they stuck with me and I just had to get them inked, in case..." my voice gets away from me and I have to clear my throat to continue. "In case you didn't make it here. In case an online chat was all we'd ever have."

Nox's eyes glisten and instead of words his response is to lean over and kiss the inked words on my skin. Then he trails his lips up my pecs until he reaches my neck. He wraps his arms around me and when his tongue flicks my ear lobe my restraint snaps. I tackle him onto the bed.

Nox's legs wrap around my hips as our desperate cocks grind together. Air rushes out of my lungs and my stomach tightens at the overwhelming pleasure of it. How many times have I fantasized about fucking against another hard dick, coming all over it and then jerking the other man off, using my own release for lubrication?

This is so much better than I'd imagined.

I kiss and lick my way along Nox's jaw and down his throat, admiring the way his skin pinks under my touch.

"Um, Adam," Nox says, pushing slightly against my shoulder to get my attention. I immediately still, propping myself up on my forearms so I can look at him, my breath coming in heavy bursts.

"Did I do something wrong? Am I fucking this up already?"

"No," Nox laughs, grabbing my ass and forcing me to thrust against him. "It's just...I don't know what you want, tonight or whatever, but I don't really want to...uh..."

"Bird, I'll never do anything you don't want. I'm happy to do whatever you're up for, so just tell me what you don't want."

I run my thumb along his jaw and hold his gaze, willing him to see that he can trust me. I would *never* hurt him like his asshole ex did.

"I don't want to bottom, if that's okay?" Nox looks so worried that I'm going to tell him it's a dealbreaker. Truth is, I'm happy to hear he wants to top. I wasn't sure how that usually gets decided, but it seems intuitive that the smaller man would want to bottom. And I've heard that some guys will refuse to top. I've fucked before, but I've never been fucked. I want it. I want everything from Nox.

"That's okay. Not that we *have* to fuck right now, but when we do I can bottom. I want to."

Nox's eyes flash with lust and he humps his cock against mine again.

"Oh yeah? Well, what do you want to do now?" Nox teases, canting his hips again and running his fingers from my stomach up to my pecs, and then roughly pinching my nipples.

"Oh fuck," I gasp as heat begins to flame in the pit of my stomach.

"You want to keep doing this?" Nox asks in a sweet voice this time, grabbing my hips and encouraging me to rut against him. "You want to shoot your load all over my cock?"

The pressure builds in the base of my cock, and in my balls as I thrust harder against him, nearly undone by the picture he just painted for me.

"God yes," I moan, biting down on the corded part of his neck. "I want to watch you come. I want our cocks to throb against each other while our release mixes and coats us both."

"Holy fuck that's hot." Nox's fingers dig hard into the skin on my hips. "Oh Jesus, oh god."

When Nox arches against me lets out a guttural moan my control snaps and I reach the point of no return, fucking our cocks together as we both pulse out our orgasms. I collapse against him as aftershocks continue to rage through me.

As soon as I can feel my limbs again I grab my shirt off the floor and do my best to clean Nox and myself up, before laying down next to him and pulling him against my chest.

It takes Nox several seconds to relax in my arms, like he's not quite sure how you're supposed to respond to cuddling. Then it hits me in the heart that Nox probably hasn't cuddled a lover before.

I've never dated anyone serious, certainly never been in love. But I usually liked the girls I fucked around with well enough to stay the night and cuddle. What can I say? tattooed as fuck, but I still love cuddles. I'm pretty sure I've seen that on a t-shirt before.

Nox

I wake up with a light, teasing touch against my hip. I shiver at the contact as I blink the blurry sleep from my eyes.

I look down to find Adam caressing and pressing light kisses to every inch of my scarred skin.

155

K M Neuhold

"You're so amazing," he murmurs when he notices me watching.

"Shut up, no I'm not," I argue with a laugh, wiggling under his touch but not really trying to get away. It feels too nice to have his lips and hands on me. Sleeping in his arms last night was beyond anything I've ever experienced. I can see where physical affection like this could become an addiction of its own. I'll happily be an Adam addict all day long.

"Yes you are, Bird. You're amazing. I'll tell you a million times until you start to believe me."

"Just come here and kiss me." I tug him up and he comes willingly, covering my body with his own and laying claim to my lips.

Too soon he pulls away, propping himself up on one arm and looking down at me with an adoring smile.

"Do you mind if we talk for a minute?"

My heart stills. I might not know much about relationships, but I know "we need to talk" is never good.

"Relax, it's nothing bad. I was just thinking that you seemed uncomfortable yesterday trying to let me know while we were fooling around that there was something you'd be uncomfortable with. I thought it would be easier to discuss preferences and boundaries now instead of in the heat of the moment next time."

"Okay. Sorry, you'd think a former prostitute would have no problem talking about sex stuff. I don't know why I'm so awkward," I lament, sitting up and putting my hands over my face. The one thing I should be good for is a good time in bed, but I'm a fucking mess.

"Hey," Adam's hands are gentle as he guides mine away from my face. "This isn't the same as what you've done before. I can understand why you might feel uncomfortable. I think it's important to have these conversations, even if they are a little weird."

I nod in agreement and take a deep breath.

"I don't want to bottom," I repeat what I told him yesterday. Nerves claw at my stomach as I wait for his response. I know he said he was cool with bottoming but maybe he's changed his mind.

"I'm okay with that. More than okay with that, if I'm being honest. I mean, if you *wanted* to switch someday I'd be happy with that, too. But if you never wanted to bottom for me, I wouldn't feel like I was missing anything."

The way Adam says it, it almost sounds like he can see a long term future for us. I cling to the hope that a man like Adam could want me for real. Could he really want me forever?

"Okay, is there anything you do or don't want?" I ask.

"I'm very open to experimentation, especially with you. So, I can't say there's much, if anything, I'd be against. Something I'd like to try sometime, if you wanted it also, is some light bondage."

"Who gets tied up?" I ask cautiously. I trust Adam, but the idea of being bound and unable to move makes me feel a little twitchy.

"I do. And then you have your way with me."

"Oh," the image sends a spike of lust through me. "Yeah, we can do that."

"Do you mind me asking, is your ass a total no-go zone? Or you just don't want to be penetrated?"

"Can we play it by ear?" I bite down on my bottom lip as memories of rough and painful fucking. The feeling of being filthy and used, completely worthless, wash over me.

"I won't ever do anything you don't want," Adam promises, trailing tender kisses along my shoulder. "I only want to make you feel good. If that means I stick to sucking you off and being a willing bottom for you, I'm more than happy with that."

I nod and give him a grateful smile.

"So, how are we playing this? Will Gage notice me sneaking out of here or do you need to create a diversion?"

"Let me kiss you a few more minutes and then we'll sneak you out, is that okay?"

"Hmmm," I pretend to think about it for a few seconds. "Yeah, I'm alright with more kissing."

Adam grabs me around the middle and pulls me over his body so I'm straddling him and then we spend the next half hour making out like horny teenagers.

Adam

Nox warm and willing in my bed and in my arms is the stuff fantasies are made of. Unfortunately, his stomach starts to growl.

"Better get you fed before you start gnawing on me," I tease.

"Why do I get the feeling you'd be kind of into that?" Nox jokes back.

"Your mouth on me is most definitely something I'd be into, and something I want to explore further in the very near future. But first, what kind of date would I be if I didn't get you fed the morning after?"

"I'm not going to argue with being fed," Nox agrees, yawning widely and stretching once I release him from my grasp. He lets out a cute little groan as he works the kinks out of his muscles.

I'm keenly aware of how easy it would be to get used to having Nox in my arms at night. I don't understand why, but it felt more right than I'd expected.

Don't get me wrong, I've always loved having the soft curves of a woman cradled against me. But, Nox's hard, slender frame with just the right amount of hair all over felt like heaven.

"So, how are we playing this?" Nox asks as he climbs out of bed and starts to slip into his clothes.

I head over to my dresser and pull on a pair

of pajama pants and then one of my Heathens Ink promo t-shirts. They were Madden's idea a few months back. I'm not sure how he came up with the slogan but it totally fits. It says 'Who needs therapy when you can get inked?' on the front, and the back simply has the shop name. These shirts have been selling like crazy and bringing in a little bit of extra income in for the shop as well. Of course, I give Madden a big cut of it since the shirts were his idea.

"I'll go out and check if the coast is clear. If Gage is out there I'll distract him and you can slip out into your own room and then come out in a few minutes."

"Okay," Nox nods, his face set in a mask of determination.

I walk over to him and put my arms around his waist pulling him in for one last chaste kiss.

"I'm sorry about this. I'm not ashamed of you in any way. I just need to find the balls to tell Gage the truth and that's really fucking hard because he's going to hate me."

"I understand," Nox assures me, picking a piece of lint off my shirt. "Now let's sneak me out of here so you can feed me."

When I step out of my bedroom I hear the television in the livingroom on. I turn to Nox and give him a silent signal and then I slip out, leaving my door slightly ajar so Nox can creep out in a minute.

Luckily, the bedrooms in my condo are

down a hall from the living room. So, as long as I can keep an eye on Gage and make sure he's not coming down the hall, Nox can make it without a problem.

"Morning," I say as I plop down on the couch beside Gage.

He eyes me with suspicion, tilting his head as he examines me.

"Ugh, is Kira here?" he asks not bothering to hide his distaste.

"What? No," I shake my head, nose wrinkling in disgust. Again, not that there was anything wrong with Kira in bed, but after her bullshit threats the other day, paired with my newfound knowledge of what it feels like to fool around with someone I like as a person, you couldn't pay me at this point to touch Kira.

"Oh," Gage tilts his head in the other direction and continues to study me. "I could swear you just got laid."

I groan and tilt my head back against the couch. Sometimes it sucks to have someone in my life who knows me so well. This would be an excellent opportunity to man up and tell him the truth, but I can't make my lips form the words.

"There are people in the world aside from Kira, in case you hadn't noticed," I snap back, hating myself for the half-truth side step.

"Sorry, Kira was your main hook-up for years, can't blame me for making an assumption."

"Believe me, I am *never* going there again."

"Thank fuck for that. Does that mean there's some rando here?"

"No, I wouldn't do that without giving you a heads up."

"Morning," Nox's voice startles me.

"Morning," I say, forcing my voice to remain as neutral as possible.

Nox gives me a shy smile, quickly schooling his features when Gage glances in his direction.

"I'm hungry. You guys want pancakes?" I offer, hating myself for playing like I didn't get the best night sleep of my life naked and wrapped around another man last night.

The distrustful look is back on Gage's face.

"I want pancakes, excuse the fuck out of me for offering to make extra."

"I'd love some," Nox says timidly.

My heart jumps in my chest. I hate this ruse. I want to have stumbled out of my bedroom hand in hand, maybe laughing at a shared joke, and go into the kitchen together, sharing touches and kisses as we cook breakfast together.

Maybe one day we could. If I can get my shit together and face Gage.

"Oh dang, I think I left my phone in your car yesterday," Nox says.

"My keys are on the table by the door," I let him know before heading into the kitchen to start breakfast.

As I mix the batter I find myself whistling a tune stuck in my head. My heart feels lighter than it has since Johnny's death and I realize the song I'm whistling is Johnny's favorite song by The Red Hot Chili Peppers.

I can't help but wonder what the conversation with Johnny would've looked like if I'd come out to him. He probably would've laughed and teased me about picking a team instead of straddling the fence. It would've been in good fun, though. Maybe all three of us could've gone out to the club after Johnny turned eighteen.

What would Johnny have thought of Nox? A wistful sadness wraps around my heart as I imagine Nox and Johnny getting to know each other, maybe even becoming good friends.

Johnny, why couldn't you have just said something? Why did you have to leave instead of giving it a chance to get better?

Nox comes into the kitchen, shaking me out of my silent musings about my brother. I look up at him and smile before I realize Nox is looking pale.

"What's wrong?"

"Your tires were slashed and someone scratched a message into your car." Nox looks like he's going to vomit admitting this to me.

"What the fuck?"

I forget about breakfast and rush downstairs to see what happened to my car. Just as Nox described my baby has three of her tires slashed and on the hood one word is carved deep into the red paint: *Mine.*

"What the fuck?" I say again.

I feel Nox behind me and when I turn to him I notice he's pale and trembling slightly.

"It'll be okay, Bird. It's nothing some new tires and paint won't fix."

"But who did it?" Nox asks in a shaky whisper, casting his gaze around the parking garage like he expects the culprit to be waiting in the shadows.

"Yeah, it's kind of weird," I agree. The only person my brain can come up with is Kira, and this seems a bit crazy even for her.

Nox sidles closer to me and motions for me to bend a little and then he whispers into my ear.

"What if it's Harrison?"

Icy fingers of dread wrap around my spine.

"How would he know you're here? There's no reason for him to suspect you'd be in Seattle. Not to mention, what would he have to gain by following you here? He got away with attempted murder, I can't imagine he'd keep coming after you and risk ending up in jail."

Nox doesn't look convinced as he continues to grip my arm for dear life.

"You're going to report this to the police, right?"

"Of course. Come on, let's head back upstairs and I'll make the call to file a police report."

CHAPTER 15

Nox

Everything Adam said about it being un-likely for Harrison to be the one behind the van-dalism made sense. But, a prickly feeling on the back of my neck keeps me from dismissing the idea all together.

When we get back up to the apartment Gage suggests Kira is the most likely culprit. He doesn't know about my psycho ex, though. And, something about the message gives me the uneasy feeling Harrison might somehow know about my date with Adam. Maybe he's here
and stalking me. Maybe he's jealous. I know he never loved me or even gave a shit, but it's easy to believe he's the 'if I can't have you, no one will' type.

"I don't see Kira doing this," Adam argues as we wait for a police officer to come by and file a report.

"Dude, she faked a pregnancy to keep you, pretended her mom had cancer to gain your sym-pathy, and told Dani she'd claw her eyes out if Dani ever touched you. Kira is two scoops of crazy."

"You have a point," Adam agrees, stroking

his beard and staring off into space.

"We didn't get to eat, you must be hungry still. I'll finish the pancakes while you wait for the police," I suggest. I'd rather make myself useful than sit around freaking myself out about Harrison.

A few minutes later I hear the buzzer and then, shortly after, the sound of the front door opening. The low rumble of a man speaking comes next.

I finish cooking the pancakes and then put them in the oven on a warm setting to keep them from getting cold before Adam finishes up with the police officer.

I head into the living room to join them. I feel like I should let the officer know about Harrison, even if it is nothing more than me being paranoid. He never gave me the impression he'd stalk me if I left him. Then again, he never gave me the impression he'd set me on fire either. Sometimes you just don't know people like you thought you did.

The police officer is kind of gorgeous. Don't get me wrong, he's got nothing on Adam. But there's something to be said for the mountain of masculinity before me. His dark hair is buzzed rather short and his bright blue eyes pop against his deeper complexion.

"Do you have any idea who might have reason to vandalize your car?" the officer asks.

"Maybe this girl I used to fool around with.

She came around the other day and was pretty pissed when I told her there was no chance in hell of us hooking up again," Adam offers and then gives him the details on Kira's full name, address, and place of work.

"It could've been my ex," I jump in.

The officer turns his attention in my direction, noticing me for the first time. When his gaze lands on my scarred arms his lips turn down in a frown.

"I'm Cas Bratton," the officer holds his hand out to greet me. "Do you want to tell me about your ex?"

"He was a piece of shit," I say with a laugh. "As far as I know, he doesn't know I'm in Seattle but I figured I'd better mention him. He tried to kill me just over a year ago."

Cas' frown deepens as he starts to scribble down the information I'm giving him.

"Thanks for the information. I'm going to make sure we look into this and let you know if we turn anything up. In the meantime, here's the case number your insurance agency will want to get the claim filed."

"Thank you so much," Adam reaches out his hand and shakes Cas'. "You look familiar, have we met before?"

"I've seen you guys at O'Malley's. My roommate, Beau, is a bartender there."

Adam's eyes light up and he casts a quick look in my direction, the implication passing silently between us. *This is the guy Beau said he's hooking up with.*

I'll have to tell Dani how sexy the room-mate is. She'll be even more eager to find a way between them.

"See you around, then. And thanks again." Adam sees him out and then follows me into the kitchen for our delayed breakfast.

I climb out of the backseat of Adam's rental car at Heathens Ink the next morning, and I still can't shake the unsettled feeling I've had since yesterday morning. I tossed and turned all night. Every time I managed to fall asleep for a few minutes I had flashback nightmares of the night Harrison tried to kill me.

I don't remember much of that night, thanks to the heroin I'm assuming. What I *do* recall is the heat clawing at my throat as I tried desperately to breathe through the smoke, and the hopeless feeling of not caring if I lived or died.

I cast a glance at Adam as he playfully messes up Gage's hair, to which Gage responds with a punch to Adam's stomach.

Maybe I finally have something to live for. It feels like I might. I'm not rushing into anything and I've got my eyes wide open. I know for Adam this is likely a bit of experimentation and fun. But I can't deny the light feeling in my chest. Or the fact that I felt cold last night trying to sleep alone. One night in Adam's arms and I'm ruined. I'm kind of okay with that.

When Adam gets bored and decides to move on, or realizes he can do *so* much better than a junkie whore like me, I'll let him go gracefully and hope we can still be friends.

"I have to put in an inventory order real quick this morning and then this afternoon I've got some appointments you can join me on. Then, I was thinking I'd let you have a shot at finally laying down some ink on skin. What do you say?"

"Really? On who?"

"On me," Adam says with a smirk.

"You really trust me to do that?"

"Sure. If you fuck up I can just get one of the other guys to cover it up," Adam assures me with a laugh.

"I'm glad there's a plan B," I chuckle. "You want me to stick with one of the other guys while you do the order or man the front desk?"

"I think Madden should have an appointment he can let you in on this morning. "

I nod and head toward Madden's work station.

"Morning," I say peeking my head in.

"Morning," Madden greets me with a smile. "You look tired this morning. Trouble sleeping?"

"Yeah, sort of," I admit. "Can I ask you something?"

"Of course," Madden sets his sketch book

down and gives me his full attention.

"How do you deal with the little voice in your head that tells you that you don't deserve your man because you're nothing but a junkie?"

"Let me guess, does that voice sound anything like your ex?"

"Little bit," I laugh.

"Tell that voice to fuck off. My shrink has me do these affirmations. It feels kind of stupid at first to look into the mirror and tell yourself you're a badass, but it does help a lot. You should try that. And, at the end of the day, remind yourself the guy you're with is an adult, capable of making his own decisions. If he didn't think you were good enough, he wouldn't be with you."

"You are so very wise."

"Just call me Yoda," Madden jokes with a wink. "So, you're already seeing someone? You've only been here two weeks, you work quick."

I feel my face heating. Am I jumping into something with Adam too fast? I know him better than I've known anyone in my life, and he knows me better than anyone. True, we only met in person for the first time two weeks ago, but that doesn't change the unique bond we have.

"I'm only teasing," Madden assures me. "I've always been a boyfriend guy myself. I hated being single and it was destructive for a while because I'd stay with shitty guys just so I wouldn't have to be single. Not that I'm saying you're jumping into something because you're afraid to be single."

"I'm not," I assure him. "I'm definitely not jumping and it has nothing to do with not wanting to be single."

"Good. And if you ever want to talk more specifics I'm here for that, too. Although, for really effective sex talk Royal might be your better option."

"I'll keep that in mind."

The day winds on uneventfully, my mind fully fixed on the thought of getting to ink Adam later. I'm a little worried about fucking up, but while I was in rehab and healing I practiced tattooing on sides of pork I picked up at the butcher. I read pig skin is almost the same as human skin, so I don't feel like a total newb. I've been agonizing over what to ink. And, I've been doing my best to tamper down my excitement at the idea of my mark on Adam's skin permanently.

The last thought has been enough to keep me at half-mast all day long.

"Ready to test your skills?" Adam asks after his last appointment leaves.

"Ready as I'll ever be." I take a deep breath to steady my nerves.

"Don't worry, it's going to be fine."

I nod and roll my shoulders back to loosen them.

"Where are we putting this?" I ask.

K M Neuhold

"I don't know what you're putting on me so it's hard to make a judgement. Wherever you think it'll fit best. You might've noticed last night my arms and most of my torso is pretty covered."

"You don't want to know what it is?" I ask incredulous.

"Nah, it'll be more fun as a surprise. So is it big?"

I let out a chuckle at the double entendre.

"I didn't realize you were a size queen," I joke and Adam gives my shoulder a little shove.

"Oh my god, you know what I meant, perv."

"The design I have in mind is fairly big. It might look pretty cool on your thigh, if you're up for it?"

"Yeah, consider me your canvas."

I nearly salivate at his words. The idea of having free reign to create lasting art all over his body is a dream come true.

I start to set up the equipment as Adam strips out of his jeans and settles into the chair in his red boxer briefs. Having him partially naked in my periphery I start to make mistakes and Adam has to call out a few corrections to my preparation.

Eventually it all gets done correctly and as I slip my hands into a pair of gloves I will them to be steady. I can't fuck this up. I know Adam said it would be okay if I did. But, I want this to be perfect.

As I set to work Adam gives me pointers

here and there, correcting my technique and complementing things I'm apparently already a natural at.

"I give up, what is it?" Adam finally asks once I have the entire outline done.

"It's a Griffin."

Adam cocks his head questioningly and I feel heat creeping into my cheeks.

"It's a half lion, half eagle and it's known for being a protector."

"I love it," Adam says, his voice slightly strained.

When I pause and look up to make sure I didn't fuck up somehow Adam catches my lips with his in a tender kiss. It's not hot and urgent like yesterday. It's a slow coupling, more of a tease than anything. But I'm still left breathless by the time he pulls back.

"You've saved my life in more ways than you'll ever know."

Adam rests his forehead against mine and a heavy silence falls between us, filled with unspoken words and unnamed emotions.

After a few seconds Adam clears his throat and sits back.

"Do you need a break or want to call it good for today and pick this back up later?"

"If you need a break that's fine, but I'm okay so far."

"Do your thing then. But don't be afraid to rest if you need it. It can take a bit until you get used to the prolonged vibrations from the machine making your hand go numb."

"I feel like there's a sex joke in there somewhere, but I'm going to leave it alone."

Adam chuckles as he leans back in the chair again and we fall into light conversation as I continue to work.

CHAPTER 16

Nox

"I know something you don't know," I taunt, leaning over the front desk.

Dani's eyes light up at the prospect of gossip.

"Oh, tell me, tell me."

"Coffee for information," I barter.

"Deal." She grabs the 'please yodel for service' sign and comes around the counter, looping her arm through mine and steering me toward the door.

"Give me a hint," Dani pesters me as we walk down the street toward the coffee shop down the street.

"It has to do with a really, *really* hot guy."

"Ooooo," Dani squeals. "Are you seeing someone?"

It's on the tip of my tongue to brag so hard about dating Adam. Or at least going on *a* date with Adam and fooling around a bit. But that wouldn't be fair to Adam. He's not ready to deal with people knowing and I agreed to keep his secret.

"No. This very muscular, blue eyed treat seems to be the roommate and apparent fuck

buddy of a certain bartender who has inspired ob-
session."

"Shut up," Dani gasps. "You met his roommate? Is he the most gorgeous man alive?"

The image of Adam's naked body taut and
sweat slicked sliding against mine as we writhe in
pleasure comes to mind and I bite back a smile.

"He's in the top five," I hedge. "And I can only
assume that when those two aren't going at it they
must sit around and argue over who's yummier.
You've gotta get on that girl, and take pictures for
me when you do."

"I'm working on it," she assures me with a
smirk as we reach the coffee shop.

We order two to go and I decide to get a
cookie for Adam as well.

"That's thoughtful of you," Dani notes.

I shrug and force my expression to remain
neutral.

As we walk down the street talking and
laughing the hairs on the back of my neck stand
up with the feeling of being watched, followed,
hunted.

A shiver runs down my spine as I try to
glance surreptitiously over my shoulder. I half
expect to see Harrison following me, ready to
attack. I don't notice anything out of the ordinary,
but I still can't shake the feeling.

When we get back to the shop I run into
Madden who takes one look at me and frowns.

"Come with me a second," he says, steering

me toward his work area.

I'm still feeling twitchy as he steers me toward the chair next to his computer, my heart is thundering in my ears and my skin continues to prickle.

"Hey, look at me," Madden instructs. "Take a few deep breaths for me." He demonstrates by holding my gaze and breathing in deeply, then holding it for several seconds before slowly releasing. "Just like that, come on."

I obey, forcing my shallow breathing to deepen, drawing the breaths all the way in and holding them for a ten count before exhaling.

After a few minutes the slow breathing takes less effort and my heart rate feels like it's returning to normal as well.

"There we go, that's a lot better," Madden praises, rubbing my back. "Have you had a panic attack before?"

"Uh, no."

"That's okay. I'm surprised you haven't with everything you've been through. Did something trigger you?"

"I felt like I was being watched, followed. I thought it might be..."

"It's okay," Madden assures me. "It's to be expected after a trauma like you've experienced. Maybe you should think about seeing a therapist?" his suggestion is gentle like he's afraid I'll flip out.

"Yeah, that wouldn't be a bad idea," I agree, rubbing my chest. I guess it's better to think that

I've got PTSD than that I'm being followed by Harrison.

Adam

"Thirsty Thursday, boss man," Royal declares with a smirk. "Finish up your shit and let's go get drinks."

"I'm coming." I wipe down my chair and log off my computer before following Royal to the front of the shop.

Everyone is waiting for me so we can enjoy our Thursday tradition of drinks at O'Malley's.

I notice Dani is wearing a low-cut tank top and some hot high heels that make her ass look fantastic.

"Those men won't know what hit them," I assure her with a wink.

"That's the plan."

"Thane and Zade are already at the bar waiting for us, let's go," Madden urges.

I fall into step beside Nox as we head down the street. My hand twitches toward his but I pull it back at the last second.

When we reach O'Malley's Zade and Thane are waiting, as promised, holding a table for us.

"Is it just me or does he get sexier every day?" Nash asks Royal with a loving smile in Zade's direction.

Royal joins in on his loving gaze, lacing his fingers through Nash's.

"You're both sexy as fuck," Royal declares

before dragging Nash into a sloppy kiss.

Zade spots them and watches with love and heat in his expression.

"I feel like the *idea* of a poly relationship is really hot, but I don't think I could do it. I don't understand how they don't get jealous."

"Those three are made for each other. But, I totally agree with you, I could never do it. I'd much rather have one person I can take care of and love for the rest of my life." My voice gets heavy as the words fall from my lips, my eyes trained on Nox the entire time.

He shivers under my gaze but his eyes are filled with longing, with just a hint of disbelief.

"You shouldn't be so nice, you're going to spoil me. You'll ruin me for other men," Nox accuses. His tone is playful but a flicker of sadness passes over his face.

"You don't need to worry about any other men."

Nox gives me a half smile and there's nothing I want more than to pull him into my arms and kiss away all his doubts. Instead I nod toward the group of our friends and Nox follows me.

"You seem exceptionally happy tonight," Dani notes, eyeing me with suspicion.

"I *am* happy. Why do I feel like people keep saying that? Am I normally mopey and I never realized it?"

"No, but there's something different about you. You're like glowy happy. It's weird."

"Good weird?" I check with a laugh.

"Of course it's good weird," Dani assures me.

I glance around in search of Nox. I wish I could keep him plastered to my side all night. I want every one of his laughs and shy looks all to myself.

I head up to the bar for a refill and there's a new bartender tonight I haven't seen before.

"Hey, do you know if the cute guy with the scars is seeing anyone?" he asks after he hands me my beer.

My hackles immediately go up and I feel my previously happy expression morphing into a scowl. The bartender laughs and puts his hands up in surrender.

"Message received."

I go to turn and trip over the outstretched leg of the man sitting at the bar.

"Oh god, I'm sorry," I apologize. I glance at his face and a sudden chill falls over me. There's something menacing and predatory in his eyes.

"It's fine," he says, his gaze lingers on me several seconds longer than I'm comfortable with. It's like he's measuring me and judging me.

I shake off the feeling and inch past him to return to my friends.

CHAPTER 17

Nox

It's weird to think how things have changed in the last five weeks since I was in Adam's tattoo chair. I was terrified last time that he'd see the extent of my scars and be disgusted. I was struggling with telling him I was Phoenix. And I was daydreaming about what his mouth must taste like.

Now, I'm sitting confidently shirtless thinking of ways I can flirt and tease while he works on me.

Not that all my nerves are gone. One thing has been plaguing me the past few weeks we've been together. Maybe it's because I haven't been in a relationship before but it feels like things are progressing strangely slow. We've spent a lot of time kissing and using our hands to get each other off. But, he hasn't once brought up or even hinted at taking things further.

"You're quiet," Adam accuses as he rolls his stool up behind me. I hear the snap of the latex gloves being slipped into place.

"Am I?" I deflect.

"Mmhmm." The deep rumble of Adam's responds sends a tingle down my spine. "Talk to me,

Bird."

I relax into the gentle sting of the needle biting into my back as Adam begins to work.

"I guess...um...I've been sort of thinking, wondering is more like, why...um..."

"Spit it out, Bird," Adam encourages.

I take a deep breath and blurt it out.

"Why haven't you pushed for more than hand jobs?"

"You said you wanted to play it by ear so I was taking things slow. I figured you'd send out the blowjob bat signal or something when you were ready to move further than hand jobs."

"What is the blowjob bat signal?" I ask with a laugh.

"It's obviously a text with an eggplant emoji and a wet tongue emoji."

"Obviously."

"Have you been stressing about this? What, you thought I was having second thoughts about being with a man or something?"

"It sounds stupid when you put it like that."

"It *is* stupid. Do you not realize how much I want you?"

Adam's words settle in my chest, warming me from the inside out.

"How much?" I ask, my voice taking on a teasing tone.

Another deep rumble comes from Adam's throat and goes straight to my dick.

"I'm going out of my mind thinking about

you. Every second of the day I want my hands and my mouth on you, tasting you, touching you. You've got me twisted in knots, Bird."

I try to control the tremble in my body caused by his words. He hasn't stopped inking me and I don't want to cause him to fuck up.

"Me too," I manage to choke out.

"Well, this got really serious," Adam laughs. "Joke time. How do you make a plumber cry?"

"How?"

"Murder his family."

"Oh my god." I try not to laugh and fail miserably. "You tell the *worst* jokes."

"Yeah, but you like me anyway."

"God help me, I do."

The needle stops buzzing for a second and I feel a quick press of Adam's lips to the back of my shoulder before he gets right back to work.

A few hours later we're back home and I'm lying in bed trying to think of an excuse to sneak into Adam's room when my phone dings with a text notification. I check it and grin like an idiot when I see it's the blowjob bat signal from Adam.

I laugh and scramble off my bed. I ease the door open and listen for signs of Gage lurking. Once I'm satisfied the coast is clear I slink out, quietly closing my door behind me, and creep to Adam's room.

As soon as I'm inside with the door closed a pair of strong arms wrap around me from behind. The rough hairs of his beard tickle the back of my neck, his breath ruffling my hair.

"So, uh, you want a blowjob?" I ask, my stomach fluttering with nerves.

It's not that I don't *want* to blow him. And, I'm sure it won't be anything like the gag-worthy, rough experience I've had in the past that left me feeling used and nauseous.

"No, I want to give *you* a blowjob."

"Oh," is all my dumbfounded brain can come up with. "No one ever has before."

"Please let me. I want to make you feel good."

"Okay," I breath out in barely a whisper, unable to gain control of my voice.

"Mmm, god I want you so bad, Bird. You're amazing," Adam murmurs against the back of my neck, hands roaming under my shirt, along my stomach.

His praise turns my blood simultaneously hot and cold. I always wanted someone to treat me like I matter, make me feel loved. But, I'm *not* amazing. I'm not someone to be coveted and desired. What will happen when Adam realizes I'm nothing special?

Before I can spend much time dwelling on my feelings of inadequacy Adam's fingers are expertly working my pants off.

I lean back into his warmth, enjoying the

scrape of his beard against my skin as he kisses my neck.

As soon as he has my pants down he palms my erection through the confining fabric of my boxer briefs.

Over the past few weeks we've become well acquainted with each other's cocks, finding the most efficient and fun ways to get each other off with our hands alone. He knows exactly what I need.

My breath hitches as his hand slips past the waistband of my briefs and wraps around my throbbing cock with a firm grip.

With a quiet moan I let my head fall back against Adam's shoulder, my arms reaching up to loop around his neck for support.

On the next upward jerk Adam teases his thumb along my slit, gathering the pre-cum pooling there.

I whine in protest when his hand disappears, but he lifts it to his lips and flicks his tongue out to taste the flavor he collected on his thumb.

"Mmm, you taste so good, Bird. I need more."

He grabs me by the waist and maneuvers me the rest of the way out of my pants and onto the bed. Then, he kneels on the floor, my bare legs on either side of his shoulders.

Adam runs his hands up my thighs, his gaze fixated on my pulsing erection. He licks his lips as he watches a drop ooze from the tip of my cock and drip toward my stomach in a long string.

"So I guess I just, uh…" Adam reaches for my cock like he's unfamiliar with it.

I can't remember what it was like giving my first blow job. It probably would've been nerve wracking but I'd gotten high first. It was the first time I got high, in fact. A guy offered me some weed. After we smoked he said I owed him for it. He said he'd be happy to take his payment out of my mouth.

I shove the unpleasant thoughts aside and focus on the loving, incredible man between my legs.

With a determined look he leans in and runs his tongue along the thick vein of my shaft, and then up to circle the crown.

I gasp and buck at the sensation. It's so much better than I imagined it would be. I thread my fingers through Adam's hair but am careful not to hold or force him. I want this to be a pleasant experience for him too. I won't thrust down his throat without warning, leaving him sputtering and gasping.

Gaining confidence with each stroke of his tongue, Adam leans further over me, wrapping his lips around my sex and swallowing me down with enthusiasm. The room is filled with the sound of sloppy sucking and uneven breathing, driving me closer to the edge with each passing second.

One of Adam's hands ventures further down, cupping and massaging my balls. The other hand slides up my torso and when his fingers brush one of my peaked nipples I nearly jackknife off the bed.

"Holy fuck, oh my god," I gasp, thighs burning with the effort it takes to keep from thrusting into the hot, tight seal of his mouth.

Adam hums encouragingly, doubling his efforts as his head bobs faster.

"Oh Jesus, Adam, I'm...I'm...unh," I gasp and push against his shoulder to warn him but he doesn't budge and I'm helpless against the wave of blissful heat that rushes through my body as Adam sucks down everything I give him.

"That was fun," Adam says with a smirk, wiping the back of his hand across his lips, his beard glistening with a mixture of saliva and my cum.

"I think you broke me," I laugh, reaching for him.

Adam comes willingly, laying down beside me and wrapping me in his arms.

His erection jabs me in the hip and I reach down to wrap my fingers around it. Adam moans and bucks into my hand.

"Do you want me to...uh," I try to force the words out. Of *course* he wants me to blow him. What kind of guy turns down getting his dick sucked? But am I ready for it? What if it changes the way I see him?

"Anything you want, Bird." Adam nuzzles into my neck, kissing and licking as he continues to fuck the narrow channel I've created for him with my fist. I lick my lips, trying to work up my nerves to just do it when another idea occurs to me instead. "Do you have lube?"

"Yeah," Adam stops thrusting and rolls away, toward his nightstand. He reaches into the top drawer and returns with a bottle of lube.

I squirt some into my hand and then use it to coat Adam's cock before I roll the other direction so my back is facing him. I ignore the moment of anxiety that surfaces at the idea he could pin me right now and take me if he wants to.

But, he doesn't. Adam waits, breathing heavily as I guide him to spoon me and then fit his erection between my legs. Then, I reach back and use my hand on his ass to get him to thrust. It only takes a second for him to see what I'm getting at and he groans against my shoulder as he takes over the movements, the head of his cock sliding against my taint and balls with each pass.

"Oh fuck that feels good. Jesus Nox, you're so sexy," he murmurs as his hands roam over my chest and stomach, and his lips continue to tease my shoulders and neck.

I'm caught off guard by how quickly my body responds to the way he moves against me. It's easy to imagine he's fucking me and my dick is responding enthusiastically.

"Oh god, Nox," Adam gasps, his fingers digging into my hips as his muscles tense and I feel his cock pulse between my legs and sticky wetness coats my thighs.

"Holy shit that was hot," he says after he catches his breath.

"Mmhmm," I agree, snuggling close to him, unconcerned about what a mess I am.

"Let's sneak a shower," Adam suggests. "Then we can come back and sleep."

I yawn and nod before slipping out of Adam's bed and pulling on my clothes to follow him to the bathroom.

My heart pounds as we tip-toe down the hall, past Gage's room, and into the bathroom. Once we're in there I let out a relieved sigh and Adam turns to start to shower. He's back seconds later, carefully undressing me and brushing kisses against my lips.

My heart is in my throat as a wave of emotions crashes over me. Every one of Adam's gestures speaks of tenderness and love, things I don't know the first thing about. He's teaching my soul about things I have no right to want. What happens when he leaves?

"What's wrong, Bird?" Adam asks, concern filling his eyes as his thumb brushes my cheek. He pulls away and a droplet of moisture clings to his skin.

"I'm okay. Just overwhelmed."

He kisses each of my cheeks before going back to check the temperature of the water and then guiding me in.

He joins me a few seconds later after he's removed his own clothes.

Adam reaches around me for his body wash and pours a generous amount into his hand and then sets to work running his soapy hands over my body in a gentle caress.

"Sex hasn't been very nice for me in the past," I confide in a whisper.

Adam stills.

"Do you want to tell me about it?"

I shrug, turning to face the shower wall so it'll be easier to talk rather than looking in his eyes.

"I'm sure it's nothing unique for a sex worker. People feel like they've paid for you and they're entitled to treat you any way they want. Most of them didn't hurt me on purpose, more like they just didn't care. I'm afraid..." I swallow and pinch my eyes closed. "I'm afraid of how I'll feel if we...*when* we..."

Adam's hands are mild as they stroke down my back in a comforting motion.

"Nox, I promise you we will *never* do anything you aren't ready for or don't want. And your pleasure will always be my top priority. I want to show you how good and beautiful it can be between people who respect and care for each other."

"You already have."

"And I always will," Adam vows.

"So, what would you want to do with me if I didn't have any weird hang-ups?" I ask. "Obviously you'd want me to blow you."

"Sure. But, what I really want is to rim you. I want my tongue and my fingers in your ass making you come so hard you see stars."

My skin heats at his words.

"Oh," I breathe. "That sounds, okay."

"Just okay?" Adam laughs.

"Better than okay," I concede. "I want you to do that. You know, whenever the mood strikes or whatever," I try to play it off casually.

"As long as you promise you'll always keep me in the loop about your feelings."

"I promise." I melt back against him and he reaches around to wash my front as we lapse into companionable silence.

After our shower, we sneak back into Adam's room and he pulls me into his arms.

Adam

"Can I tell you something I've never told anyone before?" I ask Nox as I hold him tight against my chest. After everything Nox shared with me it seems only fair that I bare myself to him as well.

"You can tell me anything."

"A few months before he overdosed, I caught Johnny high. I brushed it off, made some asshole remark about how he needed to make better life choices, then I put it out of my mind. If I'd done something then, if I'd even just checked in with him to find out what was going on..." My throat tightens as I force the words out, laying all the guilt I've been carrying at Nox's feet. He silently strokes my back, the feel of his calloused fingers against my skin is a balm on my soul. "Maybe he'd still be here if I'd been a better brother."

"Adam, you are the most incredible, giving, caring man in the world. You were young, Johnny was young, and you had no reason to think a teenager getting high once was cause for concern. If Johnny never asked for help, how were you supposed to know? I don't have to have met your brother to know there's no way he could blame you."

I let out a long breath, feeling some of my long-held tension ease.

"I've tried so hard to do right by Johnny's memory. I've done everything in my power to help anyone I've come across who could be suffering the way he did. I just wish I could have one last chance to tell him he was so loved and beg his forgiveness for not seeing the signs when I had the chance."

"I'm positive he forgives you," Nox kisses the top of my head and tightens his arms around me. "It's time you forgive yourself."

Nox

I wake up the next morning and lay in bed for a few minutes watching Adam sleep like I'm a total creeper. In my defense, he looks so sweet and peaceful.

I reach over and brush the hair from his face with a content sigh.

The idea occurs to me to do something nice for Adam. I can't believe how understanding and sweet he was last night. Not that I thought he'd push for anything I wasn't ready for or guilt me about not blowing him. But I don't have a lot of experience in my past to suggest that most guys are capable of treating people they want to fuck with any amount of respect.

I shake off the negative train of thought and quietly slip out of bed and into my clothes. I creep to the door and listen for Gage. When it's all quiet I slink out on a mission to get Adam coffee and donuts from his favorite place down the street.

I manage to make it out of the apartment silently, but as soon as I turn to lock the door behind me, my hands fly to my mouth to cover my gasp.

Attached to the door by a knife jammed deep into the wood is a picture of Adam and I kissing against his car a few weeks ago. It was the night of our first date when we kissed outside of Heathens Ink.

Written at the bottom of the picture in red Sharpie are the words: *I see you. You are MINE.*

I rip the picture down, leaving the knife embedded in the door to report to the police. Then, I hurry back to Adam's bedroom with the picture in my fist. Thank god I was the first one to step outside, if Gage had seen this...

I don't even want to think about how much

it would hurt Adam for Gage to have found out this way. Or how much it would've hurt Gage.

"Adam, wake up," I shake his shoulder.

He groans and tries to roll away.

"You have to wake up."

The urgency in my voice finally causes him to blink awake.

"What's wrong, Bird?" Adam asks, rubbing his hands over his face in an attempt to become more alert.

As soon as he sits up in bed I thrust the picture at him. If I weren't so freaked out I'd be extremely distracted by the way the sheets pool around Adam's waist leaving his beautiful, tattooed torso on full display.

"Maybe this *is* Kira. This is starting to feel like something she'd do."

I nod, not entirely convinced. I can't exactly speak to what Kira would or wouldn't do. And I also can't say that this seems like something Harrison would do. Call it a gut feeling. Then again, maybe this is PTSD like Madden said.

I take a deep breath and sit down on the edge of the bed next to Adam.

"We'd better call the police again I guess."

Adam nods in agreement running his hands through his already messy hair.

"This isn't exactly how I wanted to spend the morning," he laments as his eyes roam over me with a hungry glint.

"Me neither," I agree. I lean over and kiss the

center of his chest and then I stand up and grab him a pair of pants. "Get dressed, I'll call Officer Bratton so we can file another report. Then we're going out for a nice breakfast to try to salvage this morning."

"I kind of like it when you're all take charge like that," Adam says with a lecherous grin.

"We'll look into that more later then."

He nods in agreement and I sneak out of his room so I can call Officer Bratton and get the shitty part of the morning over with.

CHAPTER 18

Nox

"It's nice to meet you Lennox."

"Please, call me Nox," I correct, reaching out to shake the friendly doctors hand. "And it's nice to meet you too, Doctor Marvin. Madden speaks so highly of you."

"Madden is a good man. He's worked hard on his recovery."

I nod in agreement and sit in the chair across from Dr. Marvin's desk when he gestures toward it.

"I'd love to start by establishing your goals for therapy, if that's okay?"

I bite down on my bottom lip and nod in agreement.

"I...uh...want to be able to give my boyfriend a blowjob." I feel the heat creeping into my cheeks as the words escape. *I can't believe I just said that to a total stranger.*

To his credit Dr. Marvin just nods and gives me a reassuring smile.

"What's holding you back?"

"Well, I used to...do stuff like *that* for money," I admit as I squirm in the suddenly uncomfortable chair.

"How did you feel about that?"

"That's such a cliché therapist thing to ask, isn't it?" I force a laugh to ease some of the tension in my chest.

"I think it's a valid question."

I blow out a long breath.

"I felt disposable and sort of dirty. I felt like people could look at me and just tell that I would let men do things to me for money. I felt like I had no pride and no worth."

Dr. Marvin nods in understanding.

"Do you feel valued by your boyfriend?"

I nod emphatically.

"That's a good start, then. The key is going to be good communication between the two of you and working on positive self-talk. You need to forgive yourself for what you had to do in the past and know your own worth. Does that make sense?"

I nod again.

"Do you want to tell me about your scars?" He prompts.

Adam

"Why are you so fidgety today?" Madden asks, eyeing me with curiosity.

"No reason," I lie.

"It's because Nox isn't here," Royal taunts with a smirk.

I glance over my shoulder to make sure Gage isn't around.

"Shh," I scold Royal whose smile widens.

"Wait, what?" Madden's eyebrows scrunch in confusion. "He's got an appointment with the therapist I recommended, why is that making you fidgety?"

"Oh yeah, it's so reassuring to know Nox is sitting down right now with the same guy who made you ghost your boyfriend after one session. I'm feeling so much better now."

"Wait, what?" Madden asks again.

At this point Royal is nearly giddy at what amounts to me admitting there's something between Nox and me.

"I fucking knew it," Royal crows.

"Because your boyfriend can't keep his mouth shut," I grumble.

"Which one? And for the record, I prefer both their mouths open and filled with cock."

"Charming." I roll my eyes. "You know who I mean. Nash caught me off guard last year asking if I'd ever had a sex dream about a guy. I know he told you that I was really obvious about it."

Royal laughs, his eyes lighting with amusement.

"He did not tell me that, but I'm going to have to kick his ass now for keeping it from me."

"Then how'd you guess?"

"Guess what? I'm so lost right now," Madden complains.

"Adam likes the D."

I glance toward Gage's work station again.

"Would you keep it down?" I whisper.

"First, since when? Secondly, why are you so worried about your *gay* best friend finding out you're gay?" Madden asks.

"I'm not gay, I'm bi," I correct. As soon as I say the words it feels like a giant weight has been lifted. Now if only I could work up the balls to tell Gage.

"Oh, that's cool. But still, why aren't we telling Gage? And, wait, does this mean you're the guy Nox has been dating?"

"It's complicated and yes I'm seeing Nox."

"But you're worried he's going to dump you after seeing a therapist?"

"No," I snap. "I don't know. Everything is new between us, what if he decides he needs time to figure his shit out or something?"

"Then you give him time and make sure he knows you'll be waiting for him when he's ready," Madden advises in an uncharacteristically stern tone.

The bell above the door jingles and Nox walks through with an easy smile on his face.

The tight knot that's been in my chest all morning starts to ease. With one last glance over my shoulder to make sure the coast is still clear, I round the counter and sweep Nox up into a brief kiss.

"Well that's weird," Royal comments.

When I pull back from the kiss there's shock written all over Nox's face.

"Why is it weird?" I challenge without looking away from Nox.

"Um, because it was all sweet and tender and the only other times I've seen you kiss someone was when you were kissing Kira like you were trying to punish her."

Nox scowl at Royal's statement.

"I don't want to kiss anyone but you," I whisper before brushing one more kiss to his ear and then releasing him.

"Alright, everybody back to work."

"Yeah, you can't pull off 'strict boss'," Madden says shaking his head and continuing to look between Nox and me. "Want to give me some ink, Nox?"

"Uh, yeah," Nox agrees with surprise.

"You need practice," Madden reasons.

Nox

"So, you and Adam?" Madden asks as soon as we're alone.

"Um, yeah." I'm still reeling from the way he kissed me in front of Royal and Madden without warning.

"Did your meeting with Dr. Marvin go well?"

"Yeah, it was hard to talk about some of that stuff but I'm glad I did and I'm definitely going to keep going."

"Good. It helps to have someone to talk to."

"What am I inking?" I ask as Madden strips off his shirt and relaxes into the tattoo chair.

"Give me one of those cool mythical creatures you do."

I don't even have to think to know what I'm going to give him. I sit down and grab my sketch book out of my messenger bag I'd luckily left in here earlier. I flip to the page with the image I want and set to work getting it set on transfer paper so I can make an outline on his skin to work from.

"A unicorn?" he asks skeptically.

"Trust me it's going to look awesome. And did you know that early unicorn stories attribute powers to their horns that were supposed to protect against poisoning?"

Madden's expression morphs from unsure to intrigued.

"Really?"

"Yup. Unicorns are totally badass."

"Okay." He settles back. "I'm still in shock about you and Adam. I never in a million years thought he was into guys," Madden muses as I set up.

"Yeah, I don't really believe it myself. I guess I'm waiting for the other shoe to drop. He's so...and I'm all..." I wave my hands at myself in place of a descriptor.

"I have no idea what that's suppose to mean," Madden laughs.

"We don't make a lot of sense together. He's this rugged, sexy, adult man who owns a successful business and has his shit together. I'm a junkie who doesn't know my ass from a hole in the ground. I don't have any delusions about what this is and I'm okay being his experiment. It's better than never getting a chance with him at all." I shrug, pretending to be much more casual that I truly feel about the whole thing.

"Don't sell yourself short and don't underestimate Adam," Madden advises.

Adam

After his therapy session this morning and then spending a few hours with Madden, Nox seems to have a sense of calm about him I'm not used to. Not that I'm complaining, I want to find more ways to make him feel happy and comfortable every day.

Sitting on the couch with Nox, just a few inches of space between us is torture when Gage is only a few feet away on the floor. My skin feels weirdly itchy being near Nox and not able to touch him. I'm not even talking sexually, although...

Truly though, all I want is to put my arms around him and cuddle while we watch t.v.

Nox glances over at me with a shy smile and I can tell he's thinking the same thing I am.

"Oh wow, I'm crazy tired. I think I'm going to hit the hay." *Hit the hay?* Smooth, super convincing. Gage doesn't seem phased, he just grunts in acknowledgement.

I catch Nox's gaze and give a subtle jerk of my head so he knows I'm hoping he'll follow. He nods in return but stays seated for the time being.

When I get to my room I don't waste any time, stripping down and climbing into bed to wait for Nox to sneak in.

Nox's scent lingers on my sheets and pillows making my cock throb and my heart stutter. It's only been about a month since we started fooling around but Nox feels like he's a staple in my life. I feel like there's nothing I wouldn't do for him. I've never come close to feeling this way about anyone, maybe it's quick, but it feels so right.

By the time Nox slips into my room I'm going crazy with need to taste him.

"Mmmm, is that a gun or are you happy to see me?" Nox jokes, eyes fixed on my hand slowly jerking my cock, and he licks his lips.

"Come here, Bird." My voice is tight and strained.

"You need me to take care of you?"

"No."

"What *do* you want then?" Nox asks in a sultry, teasing tone.

"I want you to strip naked and then sit on my face so I can eat your ass until you come."

A beautiful blush creeps into Nox's cheeks and his breath hitches at my words.

"I don't...um..." Nox bites his bottom lip and looks at me with shy desire.

"You don't want that or no one has ever done it for you before?"

"No one has. You don't exactly pay a whore

to give them pleasure, you know?"

"You're not a whore," I growl, protective-ness rearing up inside me. Not protective against the outside world, but against the negative self-talk Nox clearly has going on. "You are a strong, amazing, fucking sexy man. And your *boyfriend* wants to tongue your ass until you can't even see straight. That cool?"

"You're my boyfriend?" Nox asks coyly.

"Fucking right I am, now strip." I give him a playful swat on the ass and he finally hurries to comply.

I lay down on my bed and wait for him, my dick achingly hard in anticipation. I've always been an ass man, even when I was only with women. I've always loved eating ass and I'm even more excited at the idea of giving this new pleasure to Nox.

When Nox's clothes are in a pile on the floor he stops and looks uncertain again.

"Please let me do this for you. I want it so badly." A bead of pre-cum leaks from the tip of my cock and onto my stomach highlighting my enthusiasm for the situation.

That seems to calm Nox somewhat and he starts to position himself. When he starts to wiggle into place his balls end up dangling oppor-tunely and I take advantage, running my tongue along his sack and eliciting a gasp.

Nox

Air rushes from my lungs as a ripple of pleasure flows through me. I lean forward to grab onto the headboard of Adam's bed to steady myself as he tongues my balls and taint.

"Am I smothering you?" I check between panting breaths.

"Mmuh," Adam mumbles, hands gripping my waist and encouraging me to ease down a little closer.

I jump at the intense sensation when Adam's tongue teases along the rim of my hole. But his hands soothe along my hips and thighs, helping me to relax and enjoy the way he devours my ass. The fervor of his licks and the sounds rumbling from his chest as he alternates between using the full flat of his tongue and trying to work the tip inside to fuck me, I can tell he's enjoying this as much as I am.

I was skeptical that he could make me come just by eating my ass, but my doubts are fading with each skillful stroke.

"Jesus, that feels so good," I moan, gripping the headboard tighter as my hips twitch against the urge to ride the hell out of his mouth.

Noticing the minute motion Adam grabs my hips and encourages me to move, to grind against him, to take my pleasure.

I don't need any further invitation and in almost no time at all my balls are aching and the heat is spreading along my skin.

"I'm close," I warn, unsure where he wants

me to finish. I don't want to nut in his hair or on his pillow if I can help it. And time is running down for me to be able to help it.

"On my face," he mumbles against my taint before carefully sucking my balls into his mouth again. The hot pressure does me in and I have to hurry to scramble back enough to do as he asked. Once I'm in position it only takes two rough jerks of my leaking cock for my orgasm to crash over me, hot ropes of release covering Adam's face.

"So fucking hot," I praise before licking my release off his face and then shoving my tongue in his mouth.

I feel Adam's arm moving between us as I use my tongue to fuck his mouth, and seconds later he tenses, moaning into my mouth as his own pleasure overtakes him.

"Was that okay?" Adam asks a few minutes later in a sleepy, satisfied voice.

"Better than okay."

Adam reaches for a dirty shirt off his floor and uses it to mop my cum off his face. *Fuck that's hot.*

"I'm going to go get cleaned up and brush my teeth. I'll be right back."

I snuggle under the sheets and inhale deeply, letting Adam's scent fill my lungs. Madden's words from earlier replay through my mind. *Don't underestimate Adam.*

He's back quickly pulling me into his arms and nuzzling against the back of my neck. It's quickly become one of my favorite sensations, the prickly scratching of his beard against the back of my neck. I wiggle closer to him and feel his semi-soft cock pressing up against my ass cheek. A few weeks ago that would've caused me to tense, thinking of the ways he could take advantage of me if he chose to. Now a sense of trust and comfort settles over me.

Adam would never hurt me.

Even as I think those words I know without a shadow of a doubt they're true.

"Night, Bird."

CHAPTER 19

Nox

It's like Déjà vu as I look up at the sound of the front door opening and I see Adam's ex strutting in like she owns the place.

"What can I do for you?" I ask in a forced pleasant tone.

"I'm here to see if Adam's changed his mind, obviously," she says with a nasty smirk.

"He hasn't, sorry you wasted your time coming all the way down here. Don't let the door hit you on the way out."

Kira let's out a vicious laugh.

"Oh, that's adorable. You think he gives a shit about you."

I bite the inside of my cheek, determined to maintain a stoic expression. There's no way in hell I'm going to raise to her bait.

She comes around the desk and invades my personal space all the while a terrifying smile is plastered on her face.

"You're nothing more than a new toy he's having fun playing with. You think this is the first time he wanted to mess around with someone new? He always comes back to me. He can't resist me. He *needs* me."

"You need to leave, please."

Kira narrows her eyes but doesn't argue this time. She spins around and kicks my messenger bag on her way past. To my surprise, she kneels and replaces the contents that spill out before continuing on her way without a backward glance.

"Please tell me I didn't just hear Kira," Dani says, peaking her head out of her work space.

"Unfortunately, you did. I got rid of her, though, no worries."

"Wow, did you have bitch repellant or something?"

"No, but maybe we should stock up in case she comes back."

Dani and I both laugh.

"I need caffeine. You coming?"

"Hell yeah."

"So when do I get one of your famous mythical beast tattoos?" Dani asks as we walk to the coffee shop.

"Anytime you want, doll."

"What will you put on me?"

"You need a siren, luring poor, unsuspecting men to their demise."

"Love it," Dani declares. "Will you do it when we get back?"

"Of course. Do you think Adam is going to let me start working on paying customers soon?"

"Probably. You're doing awesome, no reason

for him not to. Even if this is pretty fast."

I nod and my mind wanders over the past few months since I came to Seattle, to Heathens, to Adam. I can say without a doubt this has been the best part of my life so far.

I've continued to meet with Dr. Marvin over the past few weeks and while I still haven't worked up to going down on Adam or letting him fuck me, I have gotten comfortable with him playing with my ass, something I enjoy way more than I expected.

I never thought it was possible to be *this* happy, to feel so strongly that I belong somewhere.

"Nox, watch out," Dani yells, grabbing me by the back of the shirt and tugging me hard enough to bring me to the ground just as a black BMW jumps the curb where I'd been standing only a few seconds prior.

"Holy shit," I breathe as the car speeds away.

"Fuck, did you see the license plate number?"

I shake my head and try to focus on my breathing like Madden taught me. My heart is pounding out of my chest.

"Let's get back to the shop," Dani suggests as she takes my hand and helps me up.

My entire body is trembling.

"What's wrong? What happened?" Adam's voice startles me.

I blink and realize I'm back at Heathens and

instead of Dani I'm clutching Adam like my life depends on it.

"Let's get him sitting down, then I'll tell you," Dani suggests.

Adam nods in agreement and steers be back toward his office with Dani right behind us.

"Close the door please," Adam requests once we're inside.

I lower myself into the chair in front of his desk and Adam kneels down in front of me. His hands rub up and down my arms like he's trying to warm me up and I realize I'm still shivering.

"What happened?" Adam asks again.

"We were walking to get coffee and this car jumped the curb and nearly hit Nox. Dude didn't even slow down, I wouldn't be surprised if he was on something. Unfortunately, we didn't get his plate numbers," Dani explains.

"Are you okay, baby?" Adam asks gently, brushing my hair out of my face.

Just like the other day he doesn't seem concerned about Dani knowing there's something between us. That realization warms me deep inside and starts to calm my panic.

"It was Harrison's car," I force the words past my lips.

"Are you sure? Did you see the license plate?"

"I didn't see the plate, but I know it was his car. It was a black BMW, that's what Harrison drives."

K M Neuhold

Adam's expression softens.

"I understand why you'd make the connection, but there's more than one black BMW on the road," he reasons.

"But he's been following me," I argue.

Adam's brows scrunch.

"Have you seen him? We need to tell Officer Bratton this if you've actually seen him stalking you. Why didn't you tell me?"

"No, I haven't *seen* him. It's a feeling I've been having."

"Have you talked to your therapist about it?" Adam seems nervous as he asks this and I realize he thinks this is PTSD like Madden did. Maybe they're right. I have no reason to think Harrison is following me.

"No, but I will. You're right, I'm being paranoid. I just got freaked out. I'm okay now," I assure him, patting his hand and giving him a weak smile.

I glance over at Dani and see her eyes darting between Adam and me.

"No fucking way," she says as a smile spreads across her face.

"You can't say anything to Gage yet," Adam rushes to tell her.

"*That's* what you have to say about this? Are you guys *dating*?"

"Yes, we're dating. We have been for about two and a half months. Now please chill and I'm sure Nox will fulfill your need for gossip as soon as he's feeling better."

212

"Fine," Dani sighs dramatically. "I'd better get back up front, I'm supposed to have an appointment for a hood piercing in a few minutes. Let me know if you need anything." The last sentence is directed at me and I nod appreciatively.

Once she's gone I let out a long breath and lean my forehead against Adam's shoulder.

"You okay, Bird?"

"Yeah. I'm feeling kind of stupid for imagining my ex-boyfriend stalking me."

"You're not stupid. I can't imagine how scary it must've been to be hurt the way he hurt you. It's normal for your brain to be sensitive to threats now."

"Thank you," I whisper as I turn my head and kiss Adam's neck.

"For what?"

"For being good to me. For taking care of me. For everything."

"You don't need to thank me for that. It's a given."

"Not always."

"It is now."

Twenty minutes later Cas walks into Heathens Ink.

I hear an audible gasp from Dani and I have to bite the inside of my cheek to keep from laughing at her.

"Are you alright?" Cas asks as soon as he spots me.

"Just shaken up," I assure him. "I didn't get

the plate number or anything so it was probably a waste of time for you to come down here."

"It's my job," Cas reminds me with a crooked smile.

"*Dimples,*" Dani mouths at me.

"Why don't we use my office," Adam suggests before leading the way down the hall.

Cas takes my statement and I reluctantly explain that I thought it might've been Harrison, feeling silly now for having overreacted.

"I'm taking this seriously," Cas assures me as I finish my account. "I don't know if your ex is really stalking you or not, but I'm damn sure going to find out."

"Thank you."

"Just doing my job."

Adam claps Cas on the back and holds out his hand to shake. There's something behind Adam's expression that makes me feel like he's not as calm about this as he led me to believe.

Adam

That night when we get home I'm still strung pretty tight from the scare we had earlier. We called Cas to report the incident and he seemed frustrated and concerned things might be escalating. I asked if he thought Nox could be right about his ex stalking him and Cas agreed there wasn't enough evidence at this point but promised to keep an eye out and do everything possible to figure out who's causing us trouble as soon as he can.

I wait for Nox to sneak into my room that night as has become our nightly routine. And as soon as he steps through the door I'm on him, kissing and groping him as I hurry to get him naked.

I need to feel him and taste him.

Once we're both naked we fall into bed.

"I really want you to fuck me," I tell Nox between kisses.

Nox stills, looking up at me with a mix of lust and concern.

"It's okay if you don't want to," I hedge, hoping I didn't just push things too far too fast.

"It's not that I don't want to. I'm a little nervous," Nox admits, pressing a few kisses along my neck, his hands carefully exploring my chest and stomach.

"What are you nervous about?"

Nox lets out a long breath and looks me in the eyes.

"I want to make sure that it's perfect for you. I don't want to hurt you."

"You won't hurt me, Bird," I assure him. "I haven't been fucked, but I do have a dildo so I'm not a total stranger to penetration."

Lust starts to overtake wariness in his expression.

"Okay, but if *anything* doesn't feel good, even for a second I need you to promise you'll tell me."

"I promise," I agree, heart hammering in my

chest.

I pull Nox in for another kiss, our tongues tangling, hands groping. I don't miss the subtle tremble in Nox's fingers as they run over my body. I'm hoping he'll relax a little when he realizes how much I love having my ass played with. I've loved playing with my own ass at least, and I can only imagine it'll be a thousand times better to have his tongue and fingers, or *please god* his cock, inside me making me come.

After a few minutes Nox shimmies down between my legs. I part my thighs wide to grant him enough space, tilting my hips so he can have access. I'm already throbbing before he's even touched me, pre-cum dribbling from the tip of my cock onto my stomach. Nox licks it up and a hard pulse surges through me.

Nox doesn't seem to be in any rush as he places filthy open mouth kisses on my stomach and then down my thighs, He hitches my legs over his arms and continues his languid pace licking and sucking everywhere but my cock or ass.

"Please," I gasp when his tongue grazes the crease where my thigh meets my pelvis, just shy of my balls.

Mercifully, his tongue finds my hole and I let out a thankful groan.

Finally abandoning the teasing Nox licks and sucks my ass enthusiastically.

"Oh fuck that's good. Please, fuck me, I need your cock."

He hesitates and I realize there's only one way Nox will believe he's not going to hurt me.

"Hold on a second," I tell him and he stops, looking up at me with concern.

I reach toward the top drawer of my nightstand and pull out my bottle of lube and my trusty dildo. Nox's eyes widen when he sees what I have.

"I think you need a demonstration of how much you're *not* going to hurt me with your dick, let alone your fingers."

Nox licks his lips, looking both startled and intrigued in equal measure as I coat my dildo with lube and place my feet on the bed so I can lift up a little for better access. I let out a low moan as I ease the tip inside my needy hole. Nox whimpers, his eyes glued to me. He shuffles between my legs as my eyes fall closed, my breathing ragged as I start to slowly fuck myself on my toy. My hips roll as I take it deeper.

"Can I?" Nox asks in a husky voice, his hand covering mine.

"Fuck," I moan and then nod, moving my hand away and letting him take over.

He thrusts the fake cock in tentatively at first but as my moans escalate and I start to squirm, needing it harder and faster, he starts to gain confidence. With his free hand he explores again, cupping and tugging my balls.

"Jesus that's too good," I rasp as my body quakes and my nerve endings begin to spark. "Please, I want to come with *you* inside me."

Nox moans, finally seeming fully on board with this plan. He eases the toy out and I whimper at the loss.

"Condoms?"

"Top drawer."

Nox pulls away and returns with protection. He wastes no time rolling it on and then squirting a generous amount of lube into the palm of his hand and slicking himself.

And then the thick head of his cock is pushing inside me and it's *so* much better than the silicone imitation I've been getting by with.

He's careful as he fills me, so slowly I think I might lose my mind.

"Please, more. God Nox, fuck me."

He snaps his hips forward, filling me hard and fast. My cock jumps and my body spasms.

"Are you okay? Is that too hard?"

"I'm perfect, it's perfect," I assure him breathlessly, clutching at his hips to encourage him.

Finally seeming to be satisfied Nox lets go, pounding into me with an animalistic moan.

I reach down and wrap my hand around my cock, jerking myself in time with his punishing thrusts.

"Are you close?" Nox asks.

"Yeah, so close."

His next thrust pegs my prostate and my body lights up like a Christmas tree. My muscles tense as heat explodes from the pit of my stomach and through my limbs. White jets of cum streak my stomach. I can't tear my eyes away from Nox's face as his expression goes from awed to slack-jawed to fucking bliss.

I feel his dick expand in my ass and then start to pulse. For a half second I wish he wasn't wearing a condom so I could feel the heat of his cum as it fills me.

"Fuck that was good," Nox says once his body relaxes and he falls on top of me.

I wrap my arms around him and bury my nose in his hair and inhale deeply. My heart feels weirdly full, but it's not unpleasant. It feels like I never want to let Nox go. It feels like I really need to man up and tell Gage already so Nox knows how serious I am about this.

"You were *really* into that," Nox muses in a surprised voice.

"Uh, yeah?"

"I thought you might have been just saying you wanted to bottom so I wouldn't feel bad about my hang-ups."

"Why would I do that? We could've just taken penetrative sex off the table if neither of us wanted to get fucked."

"You're unreal."

"I hope that's a good thing," I chuckle.

"It's a very good thing."

"Hey, let's get out of here for the weekend," I suggest on a whim.

I'm not under any illusion that Cas will get

this stalker situation under control in a few short days. It might help Nox feel more relaxed, though. Hell, I can't deny how much the situation this afternoon frayed my nerves as well.

"How would we explain it to Gage?" Nox asks.

"Let me worry about that. Does that mean you're in?"

"Of course."

I smile and snuggle closer. An overwhelming affection for the man in my arms steals my breath.

I can't remember what my life was like before Nox. It's crazy how quickly he became the best part of every day. If it was his ex behind the wheel of that car today I'll kill him with my bare hands. He's never going to hurt Nox again. Not as long as I have something to say about it.

"You're squeezing me to death," Nox complains with a laugh.

"Sorry." I reluctantly loosen my grip a fraction and in no time Nox's breathing is slow and even.

I'm not sure how long I lay there just enjoying the feel of Nox in my arms, imagining what our future might look like as soon as I can work up the courage to tell my best friend I've been lying to him for years. Nox is worth it. He's worth anything I'd have to give up to keep him. And if it takes the rest of our lives I'm going to make sure he sees what I see in him.

CHAPTER 20

Adam

I've spent the entire morning trying to think of an excuse to give Gage to explain why Nox and I are going away for the weekend together. And for the life of me I can't come up with a damn thing. Time is running down for me to make something up because I booked a room at a bed and breakfast in a small town just outside Portland. There's no way in hell I'm missing a weekend alone with Nox. No sneaking around, no fear of creepy notes, and no clothes if I have any say in it.

I need another perspective on this so I go in search of Owen to get his advice.

"Hey man, you have a second?" I ask as I lean against the doorway of his workspace.

"Yeah, what's up?"

"Here's the situation, I want to take Nox away for the weekend but I can't figure out how to justify our absence to Gage."

Owen raises an eyebrow at me.

"I assume telling him the truth is out of the question?"

I let out a long breath and run my hand through my hair.

"I'm going to tell him soon. But I don't really want to deal with it *right* this second when I'm trying to take my boyfriend on a romantic weekend in four hours."

Owen nods in understanding and strokes his beard as he thinks.

"Oh, I know, what about a fake tattoo convention?"

"Hm, that could work. Gage wouldn't go checking into it to make sure it's real or anything. But how would I explain only taking Nox?"

"It's last minute, you can't spare anyone at the shop but Nox is only an apprentice so you figure it'll be a good learning experience for him."

"That's brilliant, and so obvious. Why didn't I think of that hours ago?"

Owen shrugs and laughs.

"You *should* tell Gage soon, though."

"As soon as we get back," I promise.

When Gage, Nox, and I pile into my car at the end of the day I take a deep breath and prepare to lie to my best friend for the millionth time.

"Hey, I forgot to mention I think I'm going to go to a tattoo convention in Portland this weekend."

"Okay, cool. You know I can hold down the fort," Gage assures me and my heart twinges. Of course Gage would take care of everything at Heathens. It's as much his shop as it is mine.

"Thanks." I reach over and pat his shoulder. "Nox, I figured I'd drag you along. It'll be a good learning experience for you."

I glance in the rearview mirror and see Nox giving me a secret smile.

"Cool," he says in a casual tone.

Nox

Not knowing what Adam has planned I'm not sure how to pack. I end up throwing a few all purpose items into my bag and figure it'll have to do.

My stomach flutters, remembering last night and how it felt to be inside Adam.

That wasn't like any sex I'd ever had before. The way our bodies fit together, the way he gasped my name as I moved inside him.

My dick starts getting hard just thinking about it.

My fingers land on a silky tie as I riffle through my clothes and I remember Adam's erotic request from a few weeks ago. He said he wanted me to tie him up and use his body.

I go from semi hard to fully tenting my pants at the thought. My blood heats as I imagine Adam's hands bound as I lick and touch. Then I imagine his cock in my mouth with him bound and at my mercy.

"Oh fuck," I gasp as my cock jerks at the thought.

I press my palm against my erection, willing myself to calm down while simultaneously thrusting a little and reveling in the friction.

A knock at my door startles me into dropping my hand.

"Almost ready?"

"Uh, yeah, one minute." I shove the tie into my bag and grab a few other items before declaring it good enough.

Adam

I feel a bit like I'm getting away with something as we cruise down the highway toward Oregon.

"So, are you going to tell me where we're going?"

"Somewhere I can spend the weekend ravaging you."

"Mmmm, that sounds nice," Nox agrees, putting his hand on my knee and giving it a little squeeze.

I cover his hand with my own and relax into the warm feeling his touch evokes.

"I've got a game to play, we'll put the music on shuffle and whatever song comes on we have to make up a story behind the writing of it."

For the next two and a half hours laughing and coming up with the most outlandish stories and sneaking small touches and kisses.

When we pull up in front of the large, blue Victorian house Nox looks up at it with excitement gleaming in his eyes.

"Are we at a Bed and Breakfast like rich people?"

I chuckle at his enthusiasm.

"I don't know about rich people, but we *are* at a bed and breakfast."

"I don't deserve this."

"Of course you do. Come on, Bird let's get our bags inside and we'll figure out something for dinner."

"Sounds good, I'm starving." Nox's stomach growls as if to prove his point.

An hour later we're settled into our room and looking through some take-out menu's given to us by the kindly old couple who run the place.

"Thai food?" I suggest.

"I've never had it, but I'm game for anything."

I place an order for a few items we can share and then settle onto the bed, opening my arms to beckon Nox in.

He comes readily, snuggling against my chest with a happy sigh. I run my fingers through his hair and he leans into my touch like a content cat.

"Hey, I know this is vacation and I shouldn't talk about work but I had an idea I wanted to run by you," Nox says after a few minutes of quiet cuddling.

"I'm all ears."

"I've been trying to think of ways to raise money for Rainbow House. I figure it can't be cheap to upkeep and the thought of them ever having to turn kids away or shut down turns my stomach. I was thinking, what if we did a day once a month at Heathens where fifty percent of profits get donated to Rainbow House? I looked it up and charitable donations are a tax write off."

"That is an amazing idea, I can't believe I never thought of that."

Nox shrugs and I notice a slight pink in his cheeks.

"I just want to help those kids."

I pull Nox close and devour his lips. I can't believe I landed such an amazing, brave, kind hearted man but I'll be damned if I'm ever letting him go.

A knock at the door interrupts us before anything can get too exciting.

"That must be dinner."

I collect our food and tip the delivery driver generously before bringing everything over to the bed and unpacking it.

When we dig in Nox makes happy noises as he tries a little of everything. For a few minutes I'm too fascinated by the sounds he's making and his facial expressions to remember to eat myself.

Nox

We take our time eating, discussing some ideas for organizing and getting the word out about fundraising days for Rainbow House. I'm thrilled Adam liked my idea because I've been thinking for weeks about how I could find a way to fundraise for the kids.

Once we're both full, we clear away the empty containers and a familiar glint sparks in Adam's eyes.

My skin heats as I remember my fantasy earlier in the day. The same fantasy Adam told me he had the first time we fooled around.

"Get on the bed, on your knees, with your hands behind your back," I command and Adam's pupils dilate with lust. "Clothes off," I add to the instructions, giving Adam a hard slap on the ass when he turns around to face the bed.

He wastes no time obeying my command, shedding his clothes and climbing onto the bed. Then, he looks over his shoulder at me. We share a hungry smile before I grab him by the hair and drag him into a bruising kiss, his body vibrating with excitement.

I release him and step behind him, running my hands over the planes of his muscles.

"I have a surprise for you," I say as I run my finger along the seam of his ass just enough to tease. "Do you want it?"

"Yes." His voice is husky and breathless.

I bend down and fish out my bag I stashed under the bed. When I stand back up I have a red, silky tie in my hand. When the material touches Adam's wrists he lets out a low moan, his ass cheeks clenching.

"You want this, don't you?" I purr as I bind his hands.

"Yes," Adam gasps.

Once I'm finished with the knot I put my hand between Adam's shoulder blades and push until he gets the hint and falls forward, ass in the air, hands bound at his lower back.

"What a pretty sight, I almost want to take a picture," I praise, running my hands along the taut globes and then spreading them wide so I can see his tight, pink hole just begging to be filled. It clenches and Adam's hips twitch no doubt seeking some sort of relief for his achingly hard cock.

I give him a hard smack, leaving a burning pink handprint on his left ass cheek.

"Don't move unless I specifically tell you to, understand?"

"Yes."

"I kind of like that." I lick my lips as my gaze travels over my man. "The only word I want to hear out of your filthy mouth is 'yes', got it?"

"Yes," Adam moans again.

I grab his thighs and force them wider and then reach between his legs and palm his sac, tugging and massaging his balls in one hand as I lean down and run the flat of my tongue up his crack and over his needy hole.

My cock throbs as the musky taste hits my

tongue.

Adam whimpers but obeys the directions I gave him not to move or speak. I've never thought much about bondage or dominance play, but I can't deny the rush it's giving me. Nor can I deny that my cock has never been this hard. It helps that Adam is so into this, his balls already pulled tight, pre-cum leaking from his slit onto the mattress below as I tease my hands all over him, my tongue working open his ass.

I reach between his legs and slowly stroke him as I fuck him with my tongue.

Adam whimpers but behaves and doesn't move or say anything. His easy acceptance of my instructions is a bone deep thrill.

I want Adam's cock in my mouth. The unexpected thought gives me pause. Am I ready to take that step?

Adam gasps as I cup his balls with my free hand and roll them in my palm.

"Flip onto your back," I demand before I can change my mind.

I untie his hands and Adam scrambles to comply, putting his hands over his head so I can bind them again. His chest is rises and falls rapidly and his flushed cock is standing at full attention. The sight takes my breath away.

I love you. The words are on the tip of my tongue but I bite them back. Adam can't possibly love me back, can he?

Instead of dwelling on that I shuffle down

between Adam's legs. I lick my lips as I run my index finger along the crown of his cock, gathering the pre-cum and spreading it.

Adam gasps and his muscles tremble, but he remains stock still.

Emboldened by the look of pained pleasure on his face and the strain of his muscles I lower myself and test the waters by slicking my tongue along the large vein that runs along the underside from base to tip.

"Yes," Adam chokes out.

His salty skin against my tongue makes my heart race and my own cock ache. I glance up at Adam's face and there's no question, this is *nothing* like what I feared it would be. His eyes are full of adoration and longing. He's looking at me like I'm the center of his universe. I *matter* to him.

Without wasting another second I wrap my lips around him and swallow him down. Even still he doesn't thrust and gag me. Adam stays still, letting me suck and lick him at my own pace.

I take my time, enjoying the weight of Adam's cock against my tongue, the feel of his taut muscles under my hands, the gasps and moans I easily elicit. Why was I so afraid of this? How could I have ever thought *this* would make me see Adam differently? Maybe it does change things because there's no way I can deny to myself how much of my heart and soul Adam owns.

"I'm close," Adam warns, the muscles in his arms straining against his bindings as I suck harder, desperate to taste his release. "Nox, oh fuck."

Adam thickens between my lips and then starts to pulse, spurts of tangy release coating my tongue and hitting the back of my throat as I work him through his orgasm.

"Oh my god, I love you," Adam mutters as I release him from my mouth.

My blood runs cold. Of course I hoped Adam might feel the same way I do, but...

I take in his disheveled and sated appearance. His hands are still secured over his head and he seems content to leave them there until I see fit to untie him. Does he mean it or is this post-orgasm haze?

I crawl over him and release his writs from the tie. He moves just enough to wrap his arms around me and pull me against his chest

"Mmmm, give me a few minutes to recover and I'll take care of you, Bird." Adam nuzzles my hair and lets out a content sigh.

My stomach is still in a tight knot but I force the worries from my mind and settle against him.

Adam

My eyes drink in the sight of the long lines of Nox's bare back bathed in the morning sun as it peeks through the curtains.

I know I freaked him out last night when I told him I loved him, but I couldn't stop the words from spilling out. My whole body was bursting with the awe and affection I feel for him.

I'm not ignorant of how difficult it was for him to go down on me. The amount of trust that had to take on his part is humbling.

And the way he dominated me...

A delighted shiver runs up my spine at the memory.

There's no doubt in my mind that Nox is the one for me. I can see a life with him. I can't shake the image of the two of us building a life together, getting married, maybe adopting a child someday. It's everything I never knew I wanted before the shy, talented man with the scarred arms walked into my tattoo shop and asked for an apprentice-ship.

I can be patient until Nox is ready to tell me he loves me back. I know he does and I can bide my time.

I waited for my Phoenix for over a year, even when I didn't realize I was waiting for him.

I loved him before I met him face to face, I know that now. I loved Nox's soul and his sense of humor. I loved his resilient spirit.

Nox stirs beside me and I take the oppor-tunity to trail a line of chaste kisses down his spine.

He hums and arches into my touch.

"You have two choices. We can stay in bed and I'll have my wicked way with you or we can be total hipster tourists and go to the farmer's market in town."

"Hmmm." Nox rolls over and yawns before stretching his arms over his head.

"You're so beautiful," I tell him as I kiss along the marred skin on his stomach.

"Why do I get the feeling you're trying to sway my decision?" Nox laughs and squirms as I dip my tongue into his belly button.

"Wow, I'm offended. Because of those libelous allegations I'm going to get dressed and go to the farmer's market without you."

"Dork." Nox pulls me in for a quick kiss before he rolls out of bed and grabs his bag. "Let's go, sexy time when we get back."

"Sounds like a plan."

"What exactly is a scone?" Nox asks as I drag him to one of the bakery booths at the farmer's market. "It looks like a flat muffin."

"Kind of," I agree. "They're delicious, trust me."

I get a few different flavors for us to share and two coffees before turning back to Nox with a smile.

We find a grassy spot to sit down away from the chaos to enjoy our breakfast.

"Okay, yeah, these are amazing," Nox moans as he shoves an orange cranberry scone into his mouth.

I almost blurt out that I love him again, but stop myself before the words are out. I don't want to push Nox too fast.

"Oh look," Nox points to something over my shoulder. I turn my head and see an art shop.

"Let's go after we finish eating. You can never have too many art supplies."

"Preach," Nox agrees with a nod.

We polish off the pastries and head to the art supply shop.

I can't get over how perfect it feels as we browse, hand in hand.

"It's nice to be out like this in public," Nox muses, gesturing to our joined hands.

My heart twinges as his words sink in.

"I'm sorry," I tug Nox closer and kiss his forehead. "When we get home, I'm going to tell Gage and we'll never have to hide again. Okay?"

"Okay."

As we continue to look around my attention snags on a gorgeous leather bound sketch book that has Nox written all over it. I grab it along with some water colors I saw Nox eyeing when we came in and head up to the register.

"What are you doing?" Nox asks.

"Getting you a present."

"Why?"

"Because I missed your birthday. Plus, it's our, what? Three-and-a-half-month anniversary. I'd be a horrible boyfriend if I didn't get you a present."

Nox laughs and his expression gets all gooey.

"Thank you."

"You don't have to thank me. I always want to put that smile on your face, Bird."

The rest of the weekend passes with the two of us in bed, only putting on pants to accept take-out orders, and getting completely lost in each other.

By the time we're in the car heading home on Sunday night I'm strategizing about how to tell Gage I've been lying to him for more than half our lives.

"You don't have to tell him if you're not ready," Nox says, reading my expression as we drive.

"I'm ready. As ready as I'll ever be, anyway," I assure him, reaching over and taking his hand.

CHAPTER 21

Adam

We're half-way up the stairs to the apartment when I realize I forgot to grab the mail. Gage never thinks of it so I'm sure it's been sitting since Friday.

"I'll meet you up there, I've gotta grab the mail."

I wave Nox ahead and turn to jog back down the stairs.

As I predicted, the mailbox is overflowing, primarily with junk mail. But as I pull everything out, something heavy tumbles out of the pile and clanks onto the floor.

I bend down to see what I dropped and still when I notice it's an engraved metal lighter. My hand trembles as I reach for it, but I pull back at the last second before I can grab it. Something in my gut is telling me this is related to the damage done to my car and the harassing note.

What if Nox was right? What if his ex is behind this? That takes things from irritating to dangerous.

I reach into my pocket and pull out my phone.

It only rings once before Cas answers.

"Everything okay?"

"I'm not sure."

"I'm right around the corner, I'll be right there."

Less than five minutes later Cas strides into the lobby of my apartment building looking concerned.

"What's wrong? Is Nox okay?" Cas asks.

"He's fine. I just found this in the mailbox." I gesture toward the lighter on the ground. "I'm worried Nox was right about this being his ex."

Cas nods and stoops down to look at the lighter.

"You could be right. Let me take this and check it for fingerprints. If need be we'll get a protective detail on him. But I need some proof before that'll be approved." He pulls a baggie out of his pocket and uses it to pick up the lighter. "I'll let you know as soon as I have something."

"Thank you." I clap him on the shoulder and then see him out.

By the time I get back upstairs Nox and Gage are in the kitchen talking about the fictitious tattoo convention.

"You took a while grabbing the mail," Nox notes. His tone is light but the concern in his eyes gives him away.

"Ran into a neighbor and talked for a few minutes," I lie. I don't want to freak him out until Cas gets a chance to check for fingerprints.

"Can I talk to you for a second, Gage?" I ask before I can lose my nerve.

"I'm just on my way out, can it wait until tomorrow?"

"Sure."

"I'm pretty tired. I'm going to take a shower and go to bed," Nox says.

With Gage standing here I can't offer to join Nox or ask him to come sleep in my bed. I smile and nod before watching him walk out of the room.

Nox

I'm annoyed and distracted. I've been making stupid little mistakes all morning while I've been working with Madden.

"Everything okay?" Madden asks, eyeing me with concern.

"Fine," I lie unconvincingly.

"Bullshit. Talk to me."

I sigh and sink down into the chair by his desk. It *would* feel better to get a second opinion.

"Adam told me he loves me."

Madden's face lights up with a smile.

"That's amazing, why do you look so bummed about it?" Then his face falls. "Oh no, do you not love him?"

"No, I *do*," I hurry to explain.

"What's the problem?"

"He said it during sex. So, I don't know if it counts and it feels like, maybe..."

"You think he only likes you for sex?" Madden guesses.

"Exactly."

"I can see why that would worry you," Madden agrees and my heart sinks. "But, I think you're reading the situation wrong. Adam's not the type of guy to say something like that unless he means it."

"He *is* the type to stay with someone for sex," I point out. "Everyone talks about how awful Kira is and he was with her for *years*."

"He wasn't *with* her. He never took her on dates or let her spend the night in his bed. It's different with you guys. I see the way he looks at you."

"Oh." The hurt I'd been carrying in my heart for days starts to thaw. "Oh." It dawns on me this could mean Adam *really* loves me.

"Talk to him about it," Madden suggests.

I nod and stand.

"Thank you." I pull Madden in for a hug before going in search of Adam.

I find Adam in his office.

"Hey, can we talk for a second?"

"Of course." He waves me in as he pushes back from his computer and stretches his neck. "Everything okay?"

"Something's been bugging me for the past

two days."

Adam's brows furrow and he opens his arms to welcome me to him.

"Come here, Bird, tell me what's bothering you."

I crawl into his lap and bury my face against the crook of his neck for a second, taking in his scent to calm my nerves.

"I love you Nox, you can tell me anything. Is this about the stalker bullshit? Or are you struggling with your addiction?"

"You love me?" I ask in awe.

"Of course, I do."

"I thought..." I take a deep breath and blow it out before finally meeting his gaze. "I thought you were saying it because of sex the other night."

Adam continues to look confused for several seconds before the problem dawns on him.

"Oh, Bird, no." He clutches me harder. "I'm sorry I made you question it, but you mean so much to me. *You,* not your body and not for sex."

A lump forms in my throat. How can this be real? How can a man like Adam feel that way about someone like me?

"What's wrong?" Adam asks, tilting my chin up so I'm looking at him again.

"You can do better than me. Maybe you think you love me now, but eventually..."

"Lennox Dalton, listen to me right now." His firm tone sends a thrill up my spine. "I will tell you this until you believe me, you are incredible.

You might have had a hard start in life, but that's what makes you so amazing. I love every scar and every blemish on your body, because they show your inconceivable strength. There are so many people out there who are fake and empty, they're shallow. You have depth and substance. You manage to have a sense of humor and a bright outlook in the face of everything. You are my hero."

"I love you," is all I manage to choke out before nuzzling my face against his chest again.

Adam's arms are a warm weight around me, anchoring me.

"Hey, I'm done with my stuff for the day. You want to get out of here?"

I nod against his shirt before pulling back.

"Okay, let me grab my bag and I'll be ready to go."

I slide off Adam's lap and make my way to Adam's workspace to get my stuff.

I pick up my messenger bag and the strap comes loose, spilling the contents all over the floor.

"Damn," I grumble as I bend down to pick everything up.

My heart stops as my hand lands on an item I definitely did *not* put in my bag.

As my luck would have it Adam chooses that exact moment to walk up behind me.

"I know how this looks but I swear on my life this isn't what it looks like," I rush to defend myself as the small baggy of white powder trembles in my hand. I want to fling it away, flush it down the toilet before it can tempt me.

"Whoa," Adam moves close and puts his hand over mine to steady me, somehow expertly slipping the temptation away with a slight of hand trick. "I know you're not using."

"You do?"

"Of course. After I missed all the signs with Johnny it's become something of an obsessive compulsive thing for me. You and I are together all the time, you never have unaccounted for disappearances, you don't have mood swings, there aren't any physical signs like dilated pupils." He looks me in the eyes, the warmth of his hand on mine is anchoring and soothing. "Are you struggling? Is that what this is?"

"No, I swear that isn't mine. I know that's the most cliché thing to say, but I don't know where those drugs came from."

Adam furrows his brow and then something seems to slowly dawn on him.

"That fucking psycho skank," he grits out before shoving the drugs in his pocket and storming out.

I jog after him trying to keep up.

"Who?" I ask when we reach his car.

"Fucking Kira. This has her fucking stink all over it," Adam grits out, getting behind the wheel while I jump into the passenger seat.

"Oh my god, yeah she stopped by here last week. She spilled my bag and then picked everything up."

"What? Why didn't you tell me?"

"I didn't want to make a big deal out of it. She came to the front desk and sort of got in my face. She totally could've slipped something into my bag."

Adam grumbles low in his throat.

"So, where are we going?"

"To tell Kira to cut the shit with those threatening notes. And...fuck!...she trashed my damn car."

"Maybe you should take a few minutes to calm down before we go over there," I suggest. I've never seen Adam so angry. He's white knuckling the steering wheel and practically vibrating with rage.

Adam

I'm vibrating with rage. Destroying my car was one thing. Whatever, insurance paid for it to be fixed, life goes on. But planting drugs in Nox's bag is over the fucking line. What if I hadn't been there when he'd found them? It's too soon to challenge his sobriety that way.

"I don't need to calm down," I argue back at Nox. "I need to find that crazy bitch and explain to her once and for all that I don't want anything to do with her."

Nox places a hand on my knee, which calms me measurably.

"I understand why you're mad, but the last

thing you need is an assault charge against a woman."

"She's not a woman, she's a demon," I grumble.

"I know, but she appears as a woman and if you tried to tell the police she was a demon you'd end up in the psyche ward."

I chuckle and a little bit more tension eases out of my body.

"Fine, I promise not to punch her. Can I at least go tell her to back the fuck off?"

"Okay," Nox agrees.

We ride in silence for the next few minutes as I drive the familiar route to Kira's apartment.

When we pull up, Nox's grip on my knee tightens for a second.

"Come on, this will be painless," I assure him.

I buzz for Kira's unit and a few seconds later her voice crackles through the intercom.

"Who is it?"

"It's Adam."

"I knew you'd come crawling back," she says before the door buzzes to let me know it's open.

"Maybe I will hit her after all," I grit out as we head inside.

"Why don't you let me talk?" Nox suggests, grabbing my arm to slow me down.

I turn to look at him and realize what it might mean to him to fight his own battle on this one.

"Okay, but if she's a total cunt I might have to jump in."

Nox nods in agreement and moves to take the lead.

I stand behind him as he knocks on the door. The way Kira's expression morphs from seductive to irate as soon as she lays eyes on Nox is worth the trip alone.

"What are you doing here?"

"I'm here to tell you to back off. Enough with the notes and the property destruction. Your little stunt with putting drugs in my bag didn't work. So, you've had your fun, you've thrown your fit, now it's time to leave Adam and I alone. Adam is my *boyfriend*, he's never coming back to you."

Kira's face begins turning red and I know an epic meltdown is about to ensue.

Sure enough, she lets out an unholy snarl and whips her attention toward me.

"He can never make you happy like I could. He can't love you like I do. He'll never be able to give you children and build a life with you. He's just a fuck toy."

I surge forward and slam my hand against the door frame to release some of the white-hot rage coursing through me.

"*You* were the fuck toy," I growl. "Don't ever get that twisted. You were nothing and he is everything. And if I ever see your face again I'm getting a restraining order against you."

Kira sniffles and then the waterworks begin.

"Adam, please,"

"We're done here." I grab Nox's arm and pull him away. There's no reasoning with Kira when she's like this, but I think I might've finally gotten through to her. If not, the restraining order will have to be the next step.

CHAPTER 22

Adam

By the time we get home my anger at Kira has simmered and all I want is to be close to Nox. It hasn't escaped my attention that I haven't had the chance to kiss him since he told me he loves me.

The apartment is empty as we step inside so I take Nox's hand and lead him to my bedroom.

"Hey, I had an idea but I don't know if you'd be into it," Nox hedges.

"If it involves you I'm into it. Tell me what you want, Bird."

"Can we sixty-nine?"

Heat spikes in the pit of my stomach.

"Hell yeah," I agree before grabbing him by the waist and dragging him into a hungry kiss.

Our tongues tangle and duel as we strip each other bare. The feel of his hot skin under my hands drives me wild.

I reach between us and take both of our erections in one hand and stroke them together as I shuffle us toward the bed.

"Let's go side by side, it's less awkward than top and bottom," I suggest as I guide Nox into bed.

He raises an eyebrow at me.

"You sound like you have experience with this."

"Not with a man. And, certainly not with anyone I've been in love with."

Nox's expression switches from slightly jealous to smug and then he climbs into bed. After a few minutes of awkwardly arranging ourselves into the correct position I'm met with the welcome sight of Nox's cock directly in front of my face.

I waste no time taking him into my throat, licking and sucking like my life depends on it. Each whimper and moan I draw from him vibrates around my cock, buried between his lips.

I'm careful not to thrust into his mouth, holding my hips still I let him take me how he's comfortable.

He uses his hand to stroke what he isn't taking in his mouth and it only takes a few minutes for a tingling at the base of my spine to start, warning me I won't last much longer. I suck him harder and deeper, as desperate for his pleasure as I am for my own.

"God, Adam, so good," Nox moans, pulling his mouth off me and stroking me, adding a little twist each time he reaches the head.

I moan around his cock as my release hits me without warning. Nox is only a few seconds behind, flooding my mouth and shouting my name.

"We need a shower," I declare as soon as my breathing returns to normal.

"Can't move, I'm dead," Nox argues.

"I've got you." I take Nox's arms and arrange them around my neck, he complies, grabbing on tight. Then I put his legs around my waist and lift him up. Nox giggles against my neck as I carry him out of the bedroom.

"When I die, will you keep my corpse and creepily cuddle it for years?"

"What? No, that's gross," I laugh.

Nox pushes out his bottom lip in an exaggerated pout.

"I thought you loved me."

"You are so fucking weird," I shake my head and blow a raspberry against his neck.

"What the fuck?"

My blood runs cold and I stop dead in my tracks. Gage is standing a few feet away, staring wide eyed at a very naked Nox wrapped around me.

"I didn't think you'd be home for hours," I respond with a light tremor in my voice. This is the last possible way I imagined coming out to Gage.

Nox is very quiet and still in my arms like he's not sure how I want to play this. It's not like I can deny what's going on. We're stark naked and I'm holding him like a baby koala and kissing his neck. I give Nox's hip a light squeeze and then set him down.

"Go hop in the shower," I whisper in his ear

and then brush a kiss to his cheek.

"You don't need me for moral support or anything?" he asks, casting a quick glance over his shoulder at Gage who's staring at me with a mixture of confusion and hurt.

"Nah, I owe him a conversation."

Nox nods and presses a quick kiss to my bare chest before inching past Gage and heading for the bathroom.

"Mind if I throw on some pants at least?" I ask Gage with a nervous laugh.

He's still silently staring at me, unnerving me. When he doesn't respond I turn back to my room and grab the first shorts I find and yank them on. I step back into the hallway to find Gage missing. My gut clenches. I can't imagine how he must be feeling. Betrayed? Confused? Pissed? All would be justified.

I check the living room first and thankfully find my best friend there, staring ahead in the dark. I approach slowly, rehearsing my defense in my mind.

"I'm not exactly sure how to do this, or like where to start," I admit, rubbing the back of my head as I stand a few feet away from him.

"How?...Are you?...Is he?..."

I let out a slow breath and sink down onto the carpet beside the couch.

"Nox and I are dating, we have been for a few months."

"Since when are you *gay*?" Gage asks, shaking

his head and squinting at me.

"I'm not gay, I'm bi," I clarify. "I've known since we were teenagers," I admit in a whisper.

Gage's eyes nearly bug out of his head and his mouth falls open.

"What the actual fuck? Are you kidding me right now? You've known for, what, sixteen goddam years that you're into guys and you never thought to say anything to your gay best friend? You never told Johnny? Maybe it would've made him feel less alone to know."

Gage's words are like a knife in my chest. I bite the inside of my cheek to control the burning behind my eyes and the tightness in the back of my throat.

"You don't think I haven't asked myself the same question?"

Gage scoffs and stands up in a quick burst pacing toward the wall and then whips around to face me.

"All this time I was stupid enough to think we were best friends. You've been a brother to me. But I've been a fucking idiot. You've been having a big laugh behind me back, haven't you?"

"No, god, not at all."

Gage grits his teeth and rubs his hands over his face.

"I get it now. I finally understand the guilt that's been eating at you since Johnny died and it's totally fucking justified. You lied to him and you lied to me. How can I ever trust you again?"

I don't trust my voice so instead I just hang my head and let his harsh words wash over me.

"That's enough, Gage. You have no idea how bad he already feels," Nox says defensively. Seconds later I feel his hand rubbing soothing circles on my back. "This has been *killing* him to hide from you, but this is the exact reaction he was afraid of."

"I can't deal with this shit right now," Gage bites out and then I hear the front door open and slam shut.

As soon as he's gone the tears start to fall. Nox is there, pulling me against his chest, his arms holding me close.

"It'll be okay." Nox's lips brush the top of my head. "He'll calm down and you two will talk it out. Everything is going to be fine."

CHAPTER 23

Nox

Gage is at the front desk settling with a cute guy whose lipstick is totally on point. The poor guy is flirting his little heart out and receiving no reaction from Gage. I've been trying to work up my courage all morning and I've decided as soon as this guy is gone I'm going for it.

"I hope I'll see you around," the guy says, lingering, clearly hoping Gage will ask for his number or show *any* sign of interest. Poor guy.

"Uh, sure, if you want more ink you know where to find me," Gage responds in a detached way.

Lipstick man's face falls but he recovers quickly enough and sashay's out the door with a swing in his hips, sure to let Gage know what he just turned down.

"Hey, can we talk?" I ask once it's the two of us.

Gage looks at me, eyes weary.

"Sure," he sighs after a minute.

"How about we go grab a drink after work and talk? I'll meet you over at O'Malley's?"

Gage nods and I turn to head back down the

hallway.

My skin prickles with that being watched feeling that's become a constant in my life recently.

I shift on my feet and lean back against the side of the bar, just next to the dark mouth of the alley. I hope it wasn't a mistake to ask Gage here to talk. What if I'm overstepping a boundary in his and Adam's friendship?

The click of a lighter coming from the alley sends a shiver down my spine. I could almost swear for a second I can smell Harrison's cologne and I gag a little.

Without warning a pair of arms wrap around me. One going around my middle, the other around my neck.

I immediately start to buck and kick but I'm no match for whoever the man is dragging me into the secluded alley. I refuse to believe what my panicked brain is telling me as I struggle for air against the arm tightening around my windpipe. *It can't be Harrison. It can't be Harrison.*

My head swims as I gasp fruitlessly. For the second time in less than two years I'm positive I'm about to die. The difference is this time I desperately want to live.

As my mind gets fuzzy and foggy I picture Adam the way he looked yesterday morning, all sleepy and happy with his arms holding me close in bed. If one more year was all the time I could have, I'm glad I at least got Adam. If nothing else I'll die knowing what it feels like to be loved.

Gage

No matter which way I come at it I can't wrap my mind around Adam being into guys. I thought we shared everything.

How many hours did I spend gutting myself open in front of him as I've mourned for Johnny? How many times when we were teenagers did we talk about people at school who we thought were hot? He could've told me. It would've been a simple statement to make.

I came out to him when we were sixteen for fuck sake. He couldn't have told me then? Or literally any day in the twelve years since?

And then to find out he's been secretly dating our roommate for months? What the fuck is that?

I can't decide which pain is gnawing harder in my gut; the betrayal or the crippling loneliness that comes with the realization that my best friend is in love with someone and I'm going to lose him.

Then guilt rears up and joins the mix. There's no reason Adam shouldn't get to find someone to make him happy just because I'm too broken to ever love again.

I don't know why I agreed to talk to Nox before smoothing things out with Adam. I guess part of me wants to vet him like a best friend should. Is he good enough for Adam? It's a moot point now, seeing that they're already in love. But it feels like the right thing to do in the situation.

I stride down the street toward the bar, trying to decide what I'm going to say to Nox. Maybe I should call Adam and tell him to meet us.

I need to apologize to him. I need to pull my head out of my ass. I need to congratulate my best friend.

Now I'm thinking about it Adam *has* been noticeably happier lately. I didn't entertain the idea he could be seeing someone because he never dated. Not serious dating anyway. He fucked around with girls like Kira, but he never showed any real interest.

As I near the bar there's a weird shift in the air. I pause and glance around, trying to place the eerie feeling that has my hair standing on end.

The sound of scuffling comes from the alley beside the bar so I creep closer to check if it's just a couple getting frisky or something more heinous.

What I see freezes my blood in my veins and kickstarts my heart.

Nox is limp with a strange man's arm around his throat. Nox's face is purplish red as the man squeezes the life out of him.

I don't have time to stop and consider a course of action. I can't remember how long the brain can be deprived of oxygen before brain damage occurs, but I don't think it's long.

Without a second thought I grab a large rock off the ground and lunge at the man.

He's too distracted to notice me so my blow lands hard and precise right to the back of his head.

The first impact is enough to get him to release his grip on Nox, whose body crumples to the ground.

I raise my arm and bring the rock down a second time just as the man spins around to face me, and I get him in the side of the head.

He goes down beside Nox.

I drop to my knees and check for a pulse on Nox before whipping out my phone.

"9-1-1, what is your emergency?"

"I need help. My friend was attacked outside of the bar, O'Malley's. Please hurry."

Adam

A loud pounding on the door startles me awake. I rub my eyes, trying to get my bearings. I must've fallen asleep on the couch when I got home from work. I slept for shit last night, worried about how I would fix things with Gage.

"Coming," I mutter loudly as I run my hands through my hair quickly and then head for the door.

My stomach plummets when I see Cas standing there in his police uniform looking concerned.

"Is Nox here?" Cas asks.

"No, why?" I choke out, terrified of what could possibly bring a police officer to my doorstep asking about Nox.

"I got a hit off the fingerprints on the lighter you found in your mailbox. It matched to three unsolved murders of prostitutes in Chicago. Two females and one male."

"Holy shit," I gasp. "It's his fucking ex, it has to be."

Cas nods in agreement and before I can even turn to slip my shoes on so we can go in search of Nox to make sure he's safe, my phone starts to ring in my pocket. An inexplicable feeling of dread washes over me when I see Gage calling.

"Hello?"

"Adam," Gage's voice sounds broken. "You need to come to the hospital."

"What?" I gasp, my heart thundering in my chest. "Are you okay?"

"It's not me, it's Nox."

"I'll be right there."

I fumble my phone as I try to shove it in my pocket. My hands are shaking too badly. Cas stoops down and picks it up and hands it back to me.

"It's Nox..."

Cas' face hardens.

"Let's go, I'll drive."

Even with Cas putting on his siren and hauling ass to the hospital it's not fast enough to calm my anxiety. Gage would've said if Nox was...

Why the fuck didn't I ask him?

It may be nothing more than a sprained ankle. But my gut is telling me it's much more serious. It's too much of a coincidence that Nox would end up in the hospital just as Cas is telling me Nox may be in real danger.

Please let him be okay.

Cas pulls his car right up to the entrance and lets me out.

"I'll meet you in there," he assures me.

I don't bother to acknowledge him I just jump out and run for the door.

"I'm here for Lennox Dalton," I say as soon as I reach the triage desk.

"And you are?" the nurse asks in a bored voice.

"I'm his boyfriend."

"I'm sorry, family only."

"He doesn't have any family," I snap "*I'm* his family."

"Adam." Gage's voice breaks through my angry haze.

"Is he okay? What happened?" I ask, hoping Gage can at least give me some idea what the fuck is going on before I lose my mind.

I take in my best friend, looking pale in the florescent lights of the hospital waiting room, and clearly shaken. This does little to calm my concerns.

"Some guy attacked him. He was choking Nox and Nox was unconscious. I knocked the guy out and called an ambulance. No one would tell me if Nox is okay. What if I was too late?"

I put my arms around my best friend and pull him close.

"He's going to be fine. He has to be." I'm not sure if I'm trying to convince myself or Gage. Maybe both of us.

"You and I both know life doesn't work that way, as much as we wish it did," Gage says against my shoulder as he hugs me tighter.

Over Gage's shoulder I see Cas walk in with an authoritative posture and approach the front desk.

"I need some information on Lennox Dalton."

I hold my breath, praying for some insight into Nox's condition.

"I'll let the doctor know," the nurse offers.

Before she can return with information two men in suits walk in and my eye catches on the police shields they have on their belts.

"Bratton," one of the men greets Cas with a smile. "What are you doing here? Thought you were off for the night."

"Yeah, my friend here needs to find out about his injured boyfriend so I thought I'd help out. You aren't by chance here about Lennox Dalton?"

"As a matter of fact, we are. Just got a

call that his attacker is awake and cleared to be brought in for questioning. Last we were told the victim...er, *Lennox*, was still unconscious but stable."

A small amount of tension leeches from my shoulders. The detectives are here to question the man I can only assume is Nox's scumbag ex. Hopefully Nox will get justice this time.

"There's an open harassment case for Nox that came back with fingerprints tied to a few unsolved murders in Chicago. Just a heads up I'm guessing the perp is our guy."

The detectives nod with determination and then head down the hall toward the patient rooms.

"Is it bad that he's still unconscious?" I ask no one in particular.

"Adam Truman," a nurse calls out.

"That's me. Is it Nox? Is he awake?"

"He's awake and asking for you."

"Oh thank fuck." My knees nearly give way from the relief flooding my body.

As soon as I'm let into Nox's room the first place my eyes land is his neck where purple bruises are forming.

"Holy shit," I gasp. "Are you okay, Bird?" I rush to his side and gently take his hand.

Aside from his neck I'm not seeing any other outward signs of injury.

"Been worse," he rasps and then gives what I'm sure is meant to be a reassuring smile.

"I was so scared, Bird." I whisper in a strained voice.

Nox lets out a quiet, hoarse laugh.

"Oh please, I'm a phoenix baby, destruction only makes me stronger. You should know that by now."

"God, I fucking love you."

"Love you," Nox's voice becomes more strained with each word and his eyelids droop. I'm guessing they gave him something for the pain that's making him tired.

"You look tired, Bird. Why don't you rest. I'm going to let Gage know you're doing alright. He's pretty worried, too."

Nox nods and falls back into the pillow. I lean over and brush a kiss against his forehead. I breath in deeply filling my lungs with Nox. I'm not a religious man but I send up a silent thanks to any deity that might want to take the credit for saving Nox's life for a second time since I've known him, and no doubt countless times before that.

When I step back out into the hall Cas and Gage are waiting.

Now that I'm clear-headed I'm able to appreciate what Gage did for Nox tonight.

I grab my best friend in a fierce hug and crush him against me.

"You saved his life. I'll never be able to thank you enough. I don't know what I would've done…"

"Of course I helped him. I don't need you to

thank me."

"I'm sorry for lying to you. I've been carrying around guilt over this for so many years. It spiraled. Every day I didn't tell you the truth it got harder. I never meant to hurt you."

"I know," Gage pats my back. "Let's forget about it. I love you man, I want you to be happy and I'm glad you found a guy who's right for you."

"Thank you."

"I guess I better start looking for a new place to live, huh?" Gage says sadly, pulling back from the hug.

"What? Why?"

"You and Nox are all couple-y now. You don't need me cramping your style. It's past time anyway. I've been leaning on you way too long. You deserve to have a life that doesn't revolve around your mopey best friend."

"My life will *always* revolve around my mopey best friend" I counter.

"Nah, you've got your man now. Go be happy. I'll still be here, I'll just be trying to prop myself up for a change."

Nox

I shift in the stiff hospital bed, trying in vain to get comfortable. I've only been here one day but I'm ready to go home.

There's a tap on the door and then it opens. Cas steps in, looking me over with concern.

"How're you feeling?"

"Awesome," I rasp quietly.

"Oh, shit, save your voice," Cas insists, pulling a chair up beside my bed.

"Did you get him?" I have to know. Harrison needs to go to prison for what he did. He needs to be locked away so he can't do it to anyone else.

"He's in custody," Cas confirms. "We're looking at him for more than his attack on you. His fingerprints tie him to three murders of prostitutes in Chicago."

"Who?"

"Amanda Viecelli, Jenna Thompson, and Josh Vasquez."

"Amanda?" I bolt up in bed, the motion causing me to become immediately light headed. I can't have heard him right.

"Yes, did you know her?"

"She was my best friend." I feel a tear rolling down my cheek.

"I'm so sorry. Did you know…?"

"I knew she died," I confirm.

"I'm so sorry. I don't know why he targeted you, or her. But, I promise you'll have justice."

"Thank you." I reach out and squeeze Cas' hand in thanks.

"Don't mention it."

Madden is the next one to visit, looking pale and stricken.

"God, Nox, I am so fucking sorry. You have no idea. I will never be able to forgive myself," he says as he eases into the chair beside my bed.

I cock my head in question, trying to save my voice and avoid the pain of talking if I can.

"I convinced you that you weren't being followed. I told you it was all in your head. I projected my PTSD onto you and because of that you didn't trust your gut about your ex stalking you."

I wave him off and then open my arms for a hug. It's not Madden's fault. I'm sure I *do* have PTSD, but it also feels good to be validated that I was being stalked.

Over the next two days all my friends visit me in the hospital. *Friends*. I have friends. I'm alive, and I have a boyfriend, a job, and *friends*.

Life couldn't get any better than this.

CHAPTER 24

Nox

Two Months Later

"Surprise!"

"Holy shit," I squeal and stumble back as all my friends jump out from behind tables at O'Malley's wearing ridiculous party hats.

Adam chuckles and then strides forward, picks me up, and spins us around once. The joy in his expression is a steep contrast from the man I first came face to face with six months ago. He's so beautiful it takes my breath away.

"Were you surprised?"

"Very surprised. What is all this?" I ask, looking around at the streamers and balloons decorating the bar.

"It's your surprise birthday party."

A rush of emotions hits me in the chest and I can't decide if I want to laugh or cry. What I *do* know is that I want to kiss the hell out of my boyfriend. I do just that, devouring his lips until we're both breathless, not giving a shit that we have an audience.

"I've never had a birthday party."

"You're going to have one every year from now on. Maybe half-birthday parties, too. Hell, I'll even try to work in as many un-birthday's as I can manage."

"I love you," I kiss him one more time before letting him set me down so I can thank the rest of my friends for being here.

Adam

My heart is full as I watch Nox flit about the party full of happiness and light. I can't bear to imagine what would've happened if I hadn't responded to his anonymous post two years ago. My life without Nox in it is unfathomable.

"Hey, thanks for inviting us," Cas says, as he approaches with Beau at his side.

"Since Beau works here I figured it was only polite," I tease. "Seriously though, I'm glad you could be here. After everything you did for Nox I consider you part of my patchwork family."

"Thank you." Cas pulls me in for a quick hug. "By the way, Kira sang like a canary. It turns out she was behind all the notes and vandalism, but Harrison was pulling the strings. He approached her in a bar after he saw you and Nox together and got her all wound up about it."

"That's so crazy. I'm glad it ended the way it did."

"Amen to that. Now if you'll excuse us, Beau has been dying for us to see about the Dani situation."

"Have fun," I give them a wink and do a mental cheer for Dani.

I notice Gage by himself at the bar, nursing a beer. What I wouldn't give to help him find peace and happiness again.

A ripple of love and lust moves through me as Nox nears me with a suggestive smirk and half-lidded eyes.

"I love that you organized all of this for me, but how late do we have to stay?" he asks.

"Why, was there something else you'd rather be doing?"

"Before I knew about this I sort of had a little something planned at home."

"Let's get out of here then."

Nox

Since the attack Adam has been exceptionally gentle with me. As much as I appreciate that, I'm more than ready to be manhandled. And, that's not the only thing I'm ready for.

Before I'd gone to meet Adam at the bar for what turned out to be my surprise party, I'd tidied up around the apartment and jumped in the shower to make sure I was squeaky clean and nicely groomed in all the necessary places. Not that I thought Adam would be opposed to my unkempt, sweaty body, but I wanted this time to be special.

Adam

The first thing I notice when Nox and I step into the apartment is rose petals on the floor. My heart gets gooey at all the trouble Nox went through to set this up.

I toe off my shoes and then follow the trail of petals down the hall toward our bedroom. I laugh out loud when I see *'Top Me?'* spelled out in flowers on the bed.

"Who says romance is dead?" Nox says from behind me.

I turn around and scoop him up into my arms.

"This is very sweet, thank you."

I carry Nox over to the bed and lay him down, covering his body with my own as I claim his lips in a slow kiss, savoring his taste.

I undress him slowly, worshiping every inch of skin I reveal.

"God, I love you so much. You're so beautiful and amazing," I murmur as I lick his neck and then kiss my way down his chest.

"I don't understand how I got so lucky, but I love you, too."

When I find myself between Nox's legs, I take the opportunity to run my tongue along his cock, savoring him.

Nox's fingers tangle in my hair as he writhes and tugs, making desperate noises in the back of his throat. Instead I head in the opposite direction, pushing his legs up so I can gain access to his hot little hole I'm hungry for.

I press the flat of my tongue against his pucker and we both moan. Grabbing his cheeks in each hand I pull them further apart. I lick and suck until his hole softens under my ministrations. Then I push my tongue inside and fuck him with it until he's shaking and begging for more.

I stop what I'm doing and reach for the lube on the top of the nightstand. After squeezing a generous dollop onto two fingers and using my thumb to spread it around I slick them through his crease, gently circling his entrance.

Nox tenses for a second, his eyes flying open and latching onto mine.

"Is this okay?" I ask, applying the barest of pressure.

Nox's breath hitches and he nods. The expression of trust in his eyes stops my heart and steals my breath.

"I've got you, Bird. And if there's *anything* you don't like, tell me and I'll stop. Got it?"

Nox nods again and then his body starts to relax as I ease the tip of my index finger inside.

"Touch yourself," I instruct.

Nox obeys, his hand going to his cock and beginning to stroke himself. As he does his channel relaxes further and I'm able to work a second finger in, coating his inner walls with lube and getting his muscles ready for intrusion.

"I want it, Adam. Please."

"Patience, Bird. I don't want to hurt you."

"I'm ready, please," he begs again, leaving my restraint hanging by a thread.

I continue prepping him while I reach for a condom and roll it on.

"Are you *sure* this is what you want?" I check again. "Because I'm perfectly happy to bottom for you for the rest of our lives."

"I need to feel you inside me," Nox insists in a breathy pant.

"I'll take care of you," I promise him as I slip my fingers out and line myself up with his entrance.

I hitch each of his legs over my arms and then carefully push inside.

As I breach the first tight ring of muscles Nox gasps and fists the sheets, his whole body going stiff.

I pull back out immediately, my heart hammering with the fear that I hurt Nox.

"Why'd you stop?" he complains, reaching for me.

"I was afraid I was hurting you."

"Only a little, I was more nervous than hurt," he assures me.

"I have an idea, let's try it a different way." I grab his hips and flip us over so Nox hovers over me. "This way you can control how fast or slow you want to take it."

Nox smiles and leans down to brush a sweet kiss against my lips.

"Thank you."

"You don't have to thank me."

He kisses me one more time before wiggling back a few inches and getting into position. I hold my cock at the base to steady it as he inches down onto me.

My hands grip his thighs as his heat engulfs me, his tight inner muscles squeezing as he descends.

"Oh my god," Nox moans once his ass is flush against my thighs. "So good."

I grunt in agreement, unable to form coherent thoughts, let alone words. I wrap my hand around his cock and jerk him as he bounces up and down, swiveling his hips and becoming more enthusiastic and bold with each stroke.

My balls draw up and heat pools in the pit of my stomach as my release encroaches.

"I'm close," I warn Nox.

"Me too," he whimpers as I speed the pace of my hand. "Oh god, oh fuck," Nox cries as he throws his head back and paints my chest with thick, white ropes of his pleasure.

The sight combined with the way his inner walls pulse around me send me over the edge, my body exploding with ecstasy.

Nox collapses beside me as we both lay sweaty and panting to catch our breath.

"Wow, I didn't know it could be like *that*."

Satisfaction and relief flood my chest as I pull Nox against me and nuzzle his hair.

"It's always good when you love and trust the person you're with. I will always make you feel good, no matter what we decide to do in bed."

Nox smiles up at me with love shinning clear in his eyes, and lays his head on my shoulder as we bask in the afterglow.

"Hey, I have one more surprise for you," I say after a few minutes.

"You're stealing my thunder," Nox complains with an exaggerated pout.

"You'll like it," I assure him before climbing out of bed and grabbing my laptop. I pull up the images I have saved and then turn the computer toward Nox.

"The Amanda Fund? What is this?"

"The idea you had a few weeks ago about donating some funds to Rainbow House, I decided to take it a step further. The first Monday of every month half the profits at Heathens will go to Rainbow House, and the third Monday they will go to a charity that helps young men and women rescued from sex trafficking."

Nox's breath catches, his hand covering his mouth as a tear rolls down his cheek.

"Thank you."

"No, *thank you*. I should be doing more to give back to people in need. If you'd like, I thought you could be in charge of the publicity and everything for this."

"I'd like that, thank you. This makes me so happy."

"I'm glad." I pull Nox in and kiss the top of his head. "All I ever want is to make you so happy you'll never want to leave me. I want to find ways to make us stronger together, always."

"Nothing can ever tear us down, we can only ever get stronger. We're forged in fire and made of strength. We're going to be together forever."

"Sounds like a plan to me, Bird. Because I don't plan on ever letting you go."

The End

MORE BY K.M.NEUHOLD

The Heathens Ink Series

➢ Rescue Me (Heathens Ink, 1). To read this story about dealing with PTSD and addiction, and finding true love during an inconvenient time: click here

➢ Going Commando (Heathens Ink,2). If you're looking for a lower angst story, you'll want to check out this sexy, fun friends-to-lovers with an epic twist! Get it Here

➢ From Ashes (Heathens Ink, 3). Don't miss this story about love in the face of deep physical and emotional scars: Click Here

➢ Shattered Pieces (Heathens Ink, 4). Grab this beautiful story about a feisty man who loves to wear lace and makeup trying his damndest to help a wounded soul heal: Click Here

➢ Inked in Vegas (Heathens Ink, 5) Join the whole crew for some fun in Las Vegas! Click HERE

➢ Flash Me (Heathens Ink, 6) Liam finally gets his men! Click HERE

The Heathens Ink Spin-off Series: Inked

➢ Unraveled (Inked, 1) And don't forget to read

the sexy, kinky friends to lovers tale! Click Here

➤ Uncomplicated (Inked, 2) Beau, the flirty bartender finally gets his HEA!

Replay Series

➤ If you missed the FREE prequel to the Replay series, get to know the rest of the band better! Click Here

➤ Face the Music (Replay, 1): click Here

➤ Play it by Ear (Replay, 2): click Here

➤ Beat of Their Own Drum (Replay, 3): Click Here

Ballsy Boys

Love porn stars? Check out the epic collaboration between K.M. and Nora Phoenix! Get a free prequel to their brand new series, and the first two books now!

➤ Ballsy (A Ballsy Boys Prequel). Meet the men who work at the hottest gay porn studio in L.A. in this FREE prequel! Click Here

➤ Rebel (Ballsy Boys, 1) If anyone can keep it casual it's a porn star and a break-up artist. Right?? Click Here

➤ Tank (Ballsy Boys, 2) Don't miss this enemies to lovers romance that will set your Kindle on fire! Click Here

➤ Heart (Ballsy Boys, 3) Like a little ménage action with your porn stars? Don't miss bad boy porn star Heart falling for not only his nerdy best friend, Mason, but also his own parole officer, Lucky! Click Here

➤ Campy (Ballsy Boys, 4) a sexy cowboy and a porn star with secrets! Grab Campy's story now! Click Here

Working Out the Kinks

➢ Stay (Working Out The Kinks, 1) What happens to a couple when one of them discovers a kink he's not so sure his partner will be into? Enjoy this super cute, low-angst puppy play story! Click Here

Stand-Alone Shorts

➢ Always You- A super steamy best friends to lovers short! A post-college weekend, a leaky ceiling, and a kiss they weren't expecting. Click Here

➢ That One Summer- A Young Adult story about first love and the one summer that changes everything. Click Here

➢ Kiss and Run- A 30k steamy, Valentine's Day novella. Click Here

ABOUT THE AUTHOR

Author K.M.Neuhold is a complete romance junkie, a total sap in every way. She started her journey as an author in new adult, MF romance, but after a chance reading of an MM book she was completely hooked on everything about lovely- and sometimes damaged- men finding their Happily Ever After together. She has a strong passion for writing characters with a lot of heart and soul, and a bit of humor as well. And she fully admits that her OCD tendencies of making sure every side character has a full backstory will likely always lead to every book having a spin-off or series. When she's not writing she's a lion tamer, an astronaut, and a superhero...just kidding, she's likely watching Netflix and snuggling with her husky while her amazing husband brings her coffee.

STALK ME

Website: authorkmneuhold.com
Email: kmneuhold@gmail.com
Instagram: @KMNeuhold
Twitter: @KMNeuhold
Bookbub
Join my Mailing List for special bonus scenes and teasers!
Facebook reader group- Neuhold's Nerds You want to be here, we have crazy amounts of fun

Made in the USA
Monee, IL
15 March 2021